TALES FROM A MOUNTAIN CAVE

Tales from a Mountain Cave

THAMES RIVER PRESS
An imprint of Wimbledon Publishing Company Limited (WPC)
Another imprint of WPC is Anthem Press (www.anthempress.com)
First published in the United Kingdom in 2013 by
THAMES RIVER PRESS
75–76 Blackfriars Road
London SE1 8HA

www.thamesriverpress.com

Original title: *Shinshaku Tono Monogatari*

Originally published in Japan by Chikuma Shobō, Tokyo

A CIP record for this book is available from the British Library.

ISBN-13: 978-0-85728-130-2

This title is also available as an ebook.

Published with the support of the Japan Foundation.

TALES FROM A MOUNTAIN CAVE

Stories from Japan's Northeast

HISASHI INOUE

TRANSLATED BY
ANGUS TURVILL

THAMES RIVER PRESS

This translation is dedicated to the indomitable spirit of the people of Japan's Northeast.

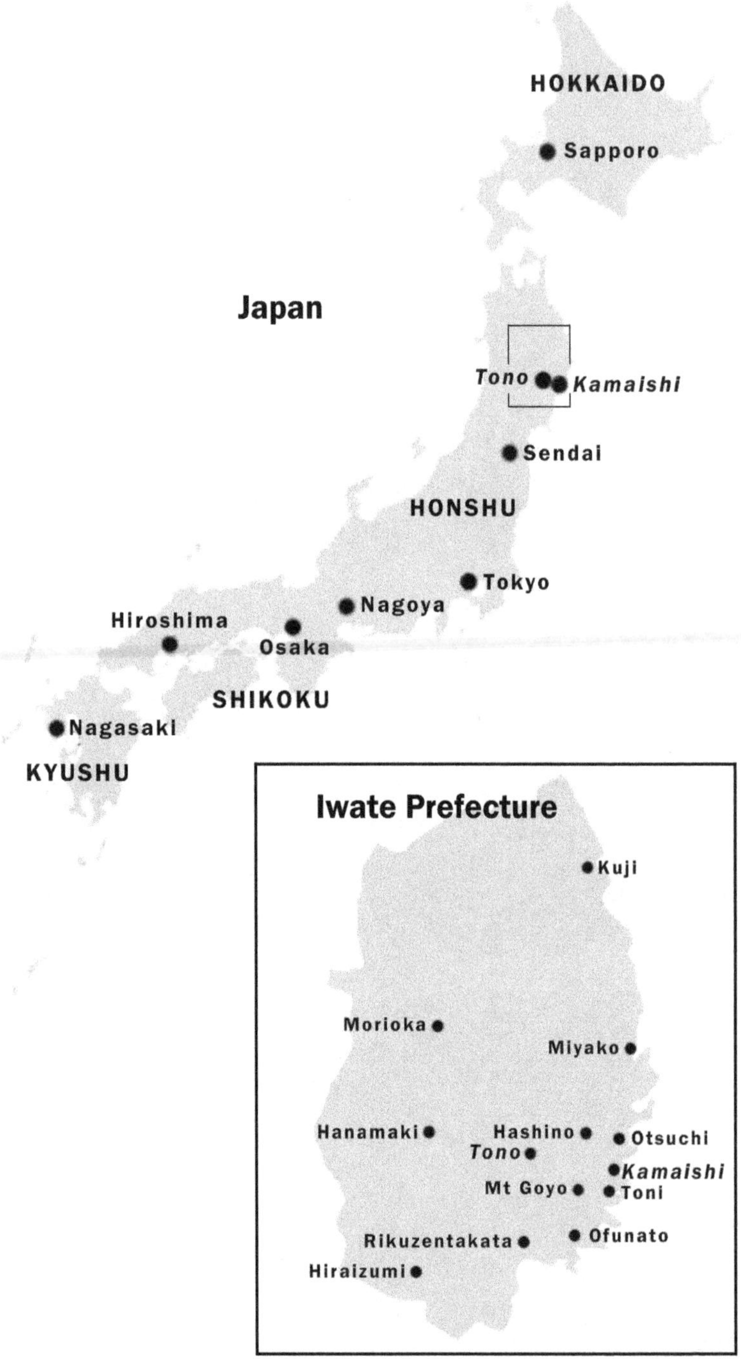

HOKKAIDO
Sapporo

Japan

Tono
Kamaishi
Sendai
HONSHU
Tokyo
Nagoya
Hiroshima
Osaka
SHIKOKU
Nagasaki
KYUSHU

Iwate Prefecture

Kuji
Morioka
Miyako
Hanamaki
Hashino
Otsuchi
Tono
Kamaishi
Mt Goyo
Toni
Rikuzentakata
Ofunato
Hiraizumi

Translator's Introduction

Tales from a Mountain Cave is set in the ports, villages, mountains and mines around Kamaishi on the coast of Iwate Prefecture, northeast Japan. Like the book's protagonist, the author Hisashi Inoue lived in Kamaishi as a young man in the 1950s and worked in the local tuberculosis sanatorium, now a hospital.

Kamaishi is a fishing port and manufacturing town. It is also an area of great natural beauty and major interest in terms of industrial history. With manganite deposits in its steep wooded mountains, the town was the starting point of Japan's modern iron and steel industry. It was here that Japan's first Western-style blast furnace was established, in 1858, and the remains of the Hashino blast furnace are currently the subject of an application for registration as a UNESCO World Heritage site. Its iron industry made Kamaishi a target in the Second World War, when it was twice bombarded by American and British warships. Civilian casualties were significant, and many prisoners of war in a local camp were also killed. Destruction has been wrought by Nature too, particularly through tsunami. Kamaishi was one of the towns worst affected by the massive tsunami that hit the northeastern coast in March 2011. One thousand two hundred and fifty residents of Kamaishi lost their lives. The building where the author lived with his mother in the 1950s was one of the many to be swept away.

Fifty kilometres inland lies Tono, a rural area strongly associated with folklore. A wide, populous basin, it has been a meeting point of people through the centuries, and a place where story-telling has thrived. The 1910 collection *Tono Monogatari* by Kunio Yanagita (the English translation *Legends of Tono* by Ronald A. Morse was first published in 1975) is regarded as the founding text of Japanese folklore. It is based on short accounts of local incidents and belief given by Kizen Sasaki (also known as Kyoseki Sasaki), himself a major figure in the development of folklore studies. *Tales from a Mountain Cave* is written with Yanagita's collection very much in mind; indeed a literal translation of the Japanese title (*Shinshaku Tono Monogatari*) might be *Variations on the Legends of Tono* (retaining Morse's rendering of *monogatari* as 'legends'). Yet while there are certainly many echoes of the earlier collection, Inoue's work is quite distinct. He takes details from the earlier book and weaves them into fuller, kinder, humorous, more modern narratives.

Translating this book has been a tremendous pleasure and I have been most fortunate to have the support of a wonderful group of people. I would like to express my thanks to Lucy North as my editor, to Etsuko Okahisa as source-text consultant, to staff of Thames River Press, especially Caelin Charge who has led the way through the publication process, and to Geraint Howells, Lydia Moëd, Polly Barton, Morgan Giles and Jonathan Lloyd-Davies as readers of the translated stories. I am also very grateful to Shigeki Sakai and Kazuyoshi Mori of Kamaishi City Board of Education, and Susumu Ogasawara and Michiyo Kikuchi of the Tono Culture Research Centre, for all the time and information they gave me, as well as to the Japan National Tourist Organisation and Japanese Local Government Centre offices in London. I would like to thank Michael Emmerich and Edward Lipsett for their interest in this project. The advice and support of all these people have been of the greatest value. I would also like to express my thanks to Shizuoka Prefecture for the motivation and opportunities given by the Shizuoka International Translation Competition, as well as to the JFL team at Regent's College.

All royalties and translation fees relating to this publication will be directed to post-tsunami support projects in association with Kamaishi City and Iwate Prefecture.

鍋の中
In the Pot

Kunio Yanagita starts his famous *Legends of Tono* as follows: 'What I have written in this book was told to me by Mr Kyoseki Sasaki, a man of Tono. I transcribed it during Mr Sasaki's occasional visits to my house, starting in February 1909. Mr Sasaki is not a good talker but he is a man of sincerity, and I wrote down precisely the impressions I received from his words. I believe there may be hundreds of such stories in the Tono area and their dissemination is greatly to be desired. In villages still more remote than Tono, there must surely be countless legends of mountain spirits and mountain people – legends that the people of the plains will shudder to hear.'

Following Yanagita's example I shall start these *Variations on the Legends of Tono* as follows: All these stories were heard from an old man called Takichi Inubuse, who lives near Tono. I wrote them down during occasional visits to his cave starting in October 1953. Inubuse is a good talker, but there's something highly dubious about him, and I myself have a tendency to exaggerate, so nothing in the book can be relied on at all. I expect there are hundreds of stories like this around Tono. I have no particular wish to hear them, but I am sure that such tales of mountain spirits and mountain people may serve to tickle the people of the plains.

I first met Inubuse about twenty years ago when I was living in Kamaishi, a port town in Iwate Prefecture, an hour's journey from Tono by train. My mother ran a bar there and I had a room upstairs. I had recently come back to Kamaishi from Tokyo, where I had been studying literature at a private university. I had only been on the course a few months, but I found it dull and I had financial problems, so I decided to suspend my studies.

I visited the employment office in Kamaishi every day in search of suitable work, and after about a month an attractive-sounding job turned up at a new government sanatorium in the nearby mountains. The sanatorium was two hours' walk from Kamaishi in the direction of Tono. The pay was low, but with working hours from nine to five and no overtime I would have the evenings to myself. If I lived at my mother's place, accommodation and food would be free and I would be able to save most of my salary towards college fees. I could study in the evenings and apply to a government university, where the fees are lower. I would try for the medical department this time. In this optimistic frame of mind I applied for the job and was lucky enough to get it.

Initially it turned out to involve much heavier labour than I had anticipated. I had expected to be responsible for book-keeping and to be wielding nothing bigger than a pen. But instead, on my first day, I was given an axe – my work for the autumn was to collect wood from the mountains as fuel for the sanatorium's boiler.

Not being used to an axe, my hands quickly grew sore. It was while I was blowing on a burst blister during my first lunch break that I suddenly heard the piercing note of a trumpet from the across the valley: it rang out as pure as a mountain stream. The trumpeter was highly accomplished – even I could tell that. I wondered who on earth it could be, playing the instrument out here in the middle of the mountains. I scanned the far side of the valley and noticed a dark hole in the hillside. Beside the hole was a human figure, and every so often the figure seemed to emit a flash of light. I guessed it must be the reflection of sunlight from the trumpet.

I was still listening intently when my lunch hour ended and the trumpet stopped. The figure disappeared into the hole. There was a distance of at least a hundred metres between us and I hadn't been able to see either the person's face or what type of clothes they wore.

How extraordinary! I thought as I returned to my work, *I would never have expected to find such a cultivated person in the depths of the Tohoku mountains!*

It wasn't just on my first day that the trumpet sounded. It rang out again the next day, and the day after that; it seemed to be a daily fixture. I couldn't identify the music precisely, but it was all classical European. Within two weeks my daily routine was firmly tied to that of the trumpeter. As soon as I heard the trumpet, I would put down my axe and open my lunch box; when the trumpet stopped I reached for my axe and stood up.

Autumn advanced and I grew used to my work. Even on a bad day I'd be gathering fifteen or sixteen bundles of fuel. In early November it rained a great deal and the mountains were often bathed in mist. On days like that my boss told me I could stay in the office and take it easy, but I put on a rubber raincoat and went out anyway. This impressed him. 'He works hard, that one,' I heard him say as I walked out the door. But it wasn't enthusiasm for work that sent me outside; I simply wanted to listen to the trumpet.

It had been drizzling all morning and the mist hung low over the valley. Towards lunchtime the rain grew heavier, and I decided that after I had listened to the trumpet I would go back to the office for the rest of the afternoon. In the meantime, I persisted with my awkward task of gathering rain-soaked firewood. When noon came, however, the trumpet did not sound. Worried that something might have happened to the trumpeter, I crossed the now deep, fast-flowing stream and tramped through sodden leaves up towards the hole on the far side of the valley. As I approached the cave I noticed purplish smoke drifting from the entrance.

'Hello?' I said nervously, standing outside.

'Who's that?' replied a quiet, rasping voice within.

'I'm from the sanatorium,' I said. 'I've been gathering firewood on the other side of the valley. Why aren't you playing your trumpet today?'

There was no reply.

'Aren't you well?' I asked.

'I suffer from neuralgia as winter approaches,' said the voice wearily, and the face of an old man appeared.at the mouth of the cave. He was leaning forward through the entrance with one hand on a log pillar. He looked up at me.

Since he lived in a mountain cave, I had imagined he'd be very dirty, but actually he was clean and neat. His long face sat tidily above a warm padded jacket. On his chin was a trim salt-and-pepper beard. His mouth protruded and his lips were thick – from playing the trumpet, I guessed. His nose was large, round, and rather red – suggesting chilblains. There was a gentle twinkle in his narrow eyes. A ski hat was stretched over his tousled hair. Somehow he reminded me of a fox.

'I always enjoy listening to your trumpet, so I was worried when I didn't hear it today. I wondered if something had happened…'

His eyes grew softer. 'That is very kind.'

'Well,' I said, 'as long as everything is okay… Goodbye!'

As I walked away the old man called after me.

'Would you like some tea?'

I looked up at the sky. The rain had turned to sleet and the idea of a hot drink was very appealing. I followed the old man into his cave. And so began our acquaintance.

The inside of the cave was as clean and tidy as the man himself. It was quite spacious too – about twenty square metres. The walls were hidden by firewood, piled up to the ceiling on all sides. And just inside the entrance was a fire, kindling snapping and flames dancing upwards. The hearth was a square cut into the wooden floor. A lamp hung from the ceiling. At the back of the cave was the old man's bedding; the trumpet lay by his pillow.

'You're a very good trumpeter,' I said, sipping my tea. The cup's rim was chipped, as rough as the blade of a saw. 'I can't really judge, but you seem better than most.'

Inubuse laughed loudly.

'I'm glad you say that,' he said. 'I used to be a professional – I was lead trumpet in an orchestra in Tokyo.'

I looked at him in astonishment. He grinned sheepishly, observing my reaction. I was baffled. He was certainly elegant in appearance and manners, and he spoke educated Japanese. But why would the lead trumpet of a Tokyo orchestra live in the middle of the mountains?

'How about another cup?' he said, passing me the kettle, and as though reading my thoughts added:

'Do you want to know why I settled here?'

I nodded. I had plenty of time. With the sleet outside, I wouldn't have to work that afternoon.

'Quite some time ago,' he said '– it must have been two or three years before the Great Kanto Earthquake of 1923 – our orchestra came on a tour of the Tohoku region.'

He took a sip of tea and wet his lips. There was a faraway look in his eyes. I warmed my hands by the fire, waiting for his next words.

'It was a time when orchestras were not common, even in Tokyo, and we had a rapturous reception at every stage of the tour. Our last performance was at Ohashi Mine, farther up from here into the mountains. We played at the Miners' Hall, and after the concert went back to our accommodation in the staff quarters. The next day we were heading back to Tokyo – by foot down the mountain, by carriage to Tono, by bus to Hanamaki, and then by train. Once we were on the train we'd be back in Tokyo in no time. It being the last night, the orchestra – about thirty of us – was having a celebration, with *sake* kindly provided by the mining company. While we were enjoying ourselves, a company official appeared with a telegram. He said it was for me. I opened it, feeling very uneasy. My apprehension proved fully justified: "Wife dangerously ill," the telegram said. "Come home."

I forgot to tell you that a month earlier I had married my landlord's daughter. We had only been together a week when I left on tour. If we had been married for ten or twenty years I might not have behaved so rashly, but as it was I decided to leave straight away.

"I must leave immediately,' I said to the man who had brought the telegram. "When I get down to the village I shall take a carriage to Tono. Would you be so kind as to write a note of introduction to the carriage owner?"

The man tried to stop me.

"It's dangerous to go down in the dark," he said. "There are still wolves in these mountains. They come out onto the road at night. And further up there are Mountain Men. If they catch you, you won't get back alive. Luckily for me, I've never come across one, but..."

My colleagues as well did their best to persuade me to wait until morning.

"It's only natural to feel you can't stay here doing nothing," they said. "We understand that. But it'll be dangerous to go alone. Wait until tomorrow when we all go. You'll be a day later in Tokyo, but it'll be much safer."

I didn't listen. What if my wife were to die during that extra day? I had to reach her while she was still alive. Seeing me would make her happy – she might even recover. I had to go immediately.

I set off down the mountain at about nine p.m. I had my trumpet case tucked firmly under my left arm and in my right hand I held a lantern, which the official had lent me. It was a twelve-kilometre walk down a mountain path to the village.

It was a pitch-black, moonless night, and there was nothing to guide me but the lantern. After some two miles' descent, the lantern's flame suddenly died. I had no idea what to do. I didn't smoke, so I had no matches to relight it. But I realised there was no sense in wasting time, so I carried on through the darkness, carefully checking my foothold at each step. As I carried on walking, suddenly everything around me grew lighter. Snow was falling. Its brightness helped me see where I was putting my feet, so I walked swiftly on, hoping to make up lost time. But then a wind got up, whipping the snow through the air. Flakes the size of cherry-blossom petals swept towards me from all directions. People say snow is silent, but I could hear it: *sa, sa, sa, kasa-kasa.* I stared dumbfounded as millions of snowflakes swirled around me. I began to feel that rather than the snow falling, I myself was rising into the sky. I was terrified.

I hurried blindly down the path, trying not to look upwards. Every so often I heard the blood-chilling howls of wolves in the distance. I made sure to go in the opposite direction – not only out of fear, but because I thought the village must be located away from the deep mountains where the wolves were sure to be. But then I noticed something strange: the path was getting narrower. It should be getting wider as I neared the village, but the further I walked the narrower it grew.

I was frantic. I looked at my watch. Both hands were pointing upwards – midnight. I had been walking for three hours; the distance to the village from the mine was twelve kilometres. The village lights should have been in sight by now, but there was no sign of the village at all. I shuddered. Fear clenched my guts. I was entirely lost. I stopped and tried to think, but the lack of movement only aggravated my disquiet. I walked aimlessly on, my shoulders heaving at each breath. I chose a direction at random and, throwing the useless lantern to one side, turned up the collar of my coat and walked straight on for a full thirty minutes.

There is nothing so deceptive as progress through snow. People think they're walking in a straight line, but most veer a little to the left or right and end up walking in a large circle back to where they started. That is exactly what happened to me. After walking for half an hour I noticed something dark against the unblemished whiteness of the snow. I reached down for it and was horrified to find it was the lantern I had earlier discarded. Utterly exhausted and dispirited I slumped down onto the snow.

"I can't go on," I thought. "I shall stay here and freeze to death."

My mouth was dry. I spooned snow up with my hands and crammed it into my mouth. For no particular reason I looked to my right. My throat contracted and involuntarily I spat out the snow. There was a light – not far away.

"That wasn't there before," I thought. "But whatever light it is, I'm saved!"

I waded knee-deep through the snow towards the light and before long I came to a house. The left half was in darkness but on the right a warm orange glow shone through the tightly closed *shoji* screen. I crossed the tiny garden and approached the house.

"Who's that?" said a young woman's voice inside.

"I am a traveller in distress," I said desperately. "I've lost my way in the snow. Please let me spend the night!"

The screen door clattered open.

A lovely woman of twenty-six or so appeared. She looked ill-nourished, but there was something refined about her.

"How terrible for you," she said, kneeling on the veranda, bowing gently.

I looked through the open screen to the room inside. In the middle of the wooden floor was a hearth surrounded by seating mats. A fire was burning and above the fire was a large, steaming pot.

"I am very sorry to ask," I said, "but could you possibly give me something to eat as well? Of course, I shall pay you."

The woman knelt straight and tense.

"I should very much like to help you," she said, "but I can say nothing without asking my husband."

"And where is he...?"

"He is in the woods at the moment. He is a very jealous man. I cannot imagine what he might do if I were to let a man in to stay the night without asking him first."

"Well, of course if I was a lover he'd be angry. But you and I have never met before. I am lost and came here by chance. I'm sure he'd understand if you explained."

The woman shook her head.

"He would certainly not understand. I am very sorry, but please could you wait outside until he returns."

The woman went back inside, but she didn't fully close the screen behind her – a small concession to me, I suppose. Delicious smells wafted out from the cooking pot.

After a while the woman stood up and went out to the back of the house. She was gone for some time. My hunger was growing – all I'd had since midday was some *sake* and a piece of dried fish. Eventually, I ran up to the veranda, took off my shoes and stole in towards the hearth, desperate to sneak a mouthful of whatever was in the pot. I lifted the lid and looked inside. I froze with horror – in the pot was a baby, simmered to a deep shade of purple.

"Quite a surprise for you, I suppose!" It was the woman's voice. She had quietly returned and was now standing close by in the unlit half of the house. There was a hatchet in her hand.

"Please forgive me!" I said. "I meant no harm. I'm just very hungry."

The woman slowly raised the hatchet above her head.

"I'm so sorry!" I said. "I'll leave straight away. I won't tell anyone of what I saw."

The woman swung the hatchet down. A thick piece of firewood split in two on the earthen floor at her feet. She looked at me and smiled.

"That is not a human baby," she said. "It's a monkey."

Monkeys are hairy. There was no hair on whatever was in the pot.

"I skinned it," she said.

But why a monkey?

"Monkey soup is a highly effective remedy for tuberculosis," she said. "The soup from one large pot will go for twenty or thirty yen in town."

On reflection, the head in the pot had been too small for a human baby.

"What happens to the meat?" I asked, shifting back onto the veranda.

"We eat it," the woman answered simply. "Monkey meat is delicious. It's tender and lean." She frowned. "At first I hated the idea. I could not bring myself to touch it with my chopsticks."

"You're not from this area, are you?" I said. "You must be from Tokyo…"

Without answering, she climbed up on to the wooden floor and put the newly chopped firewood by the side of the hearth.

"Why is such a beautiful woman living in such a place, eating m…?"

"Shh!" she said sharply. "My husband is back!"

The woman stood up and closed the screen firmly between us. I listened. I could hear the panting of a dog. It was getting closer. Then came the sound of tramping snowshoes. Suddenly the panting grew louder and a white dog the size of a bear jumped into the garden barking at me ferociously.

The screen opened and the woman appeared again.

"Shiro! Be quiet!"

Having calmed the dog, she shouted a greeting across the garden to her husband.

"*O-kaeri nasai!*"

I followed her gaze and saw a man stepping into the garden. He was wearing a sleeveless bearskin jacket and a bamboo snow-hat. A long straight knife hung from his belt and in his right hand was a gleaming black hunting rifle. Though not tall, he was broad-shouldered and powerfully built.

"Who's this?" he said pointing his rifle at the end of my nose.

"He says he lost his way," the woman said. "He asked if he could stay the night. I told him I could not reply until you came home."

I knelt in the snow and bowed my head.

"Please let me stay one night. I shall leave early in the morning. I shall be no trouble and of course I shall pay you."

The man looked me over for a while. His eyes were cruel – cold, half-dead, like a snake's eyes.

"All right," the man said, agreeing far more readily than I had expected. "Give him some food. He can sleep in the shed."

The woman showed me to the shed. It was full of neatly stowed bird-nets, barrels, and straw matting. She arranged some planks on the ground, on top of which she laid some matting and an old futon from the house. Finally she gave me a wooden bowl of millet gruel.

"Thank you very much," I said.

She left without a word. As she disappeared I glimpsed the shadow of the man outside. Under his observation she couldn't have spoken even if she'd wanted to. I ate the gruel, curled up in the futon, and fell asleep.'

Inubuse placed some brushwood on the fire and then looked steadily at my face.

'Is that all?' I protested. 'Is that the end of the story?'

'Calm down,' he said. 'That is just the beginning.'

He balanced two thick logs on top of the brightly burning brushwood.

'When dawn was near,' he continued, 'I was awoken by a cold wind on my face. Somebody was standing beside my futon.

"Wh-Who's that?" I stammered, hurriedly sitting up.

It was the woman. She put a finger to her lips and crouched down beside me. She was wearing nightclothes. Her collar was open and through the darkness I could make out the curves of her full white breasts.

"I want to ask something of you," she said.

She felt my eyes on her and adjusted her collar.

"As you supposed, I am from Tokyo. I was brought up in Yotsuya. One day when I was eighteen I went to Asakusa with a friend, and there I was abducted by the man who is now my husband."

"Abducted…?"

"Yes. He was a showman. His stunt was to eat live chickens and snakes. He noticed me in the audience that day, and while I was waiting for my friend after the show he suddenly hit me over the head. I fell to the ground and everything went blank."

"What an appalling man!"

"The next thing I knew, I was on a train. He had thrown up his job at the show that same afternoon and he was taking me back to his home here in the mountains. I have been here ever since. I have constantly looked out for any chance to escape and four or five times I have actually tried to get away. But he has caught me each time, just when I was a hair's breadth from freedom."

The woman turned around, loosened her collar and let her garment slide down her back. The pale pre-dawn light revealed an awful sight. Deep burn marks ran across her white back, like muddy tracks across melting snow.

"Each time he caught me, he punished me with burning embers."

"I'll do whatever I can for you," I said. "You saved me last night. Now it's my turn to save you. Should we escape together?"

Adjusting her collar again, she turned back towards me and shook her head.

"I would slow you down and we would be caught."

"So what would you like me to do?"

"When you get to Tokyo, please contact my family in Yotsuya. Tell them I am still alive. Tell them to ask the police to come and save me."

"Of course I will," I said emphatically. "That is the very least I can do."

I asked her name and her family's address, and memorised them carefully.

"Oh, I forgot," she said loudly, as she stood up.

"Shh!" I said. "Your husband may hear... What did you forget?"

The woman knelt again, sighing deeply.

"He may be intending to kill you," she said.

"Wh-What?"

"You must be careful. If at breakfast he offers to go with you to the village, it means that he wants to kill you on the way..."

As fear compounded with the chill of the morning, my teeth began to chatter uncontrollably.

"There will be only one way to save yourself," she said. "About eight kilometres on the path from here you will pass a *jizo* statue. Beyond that the mountainside is thick with bamboo grass. When you get there you must find an opportunity to slide down the hill."

"And then?"

"At the bottom of the slope you will find another path. Follow that path a hundred metres and you will reach a temple called Shinmyoji. If you can get into the temple you will be all right. Not even my husband will chase you inside. You can ask someone from the temple to take you to the village – it is less than four kilometres from there."

"Shinmyoji. Shinmyoji." I repeated the temple's name again and again, to lodge it firmly in my memory.

"Please do your best to get away – for my sake as well as for your own. I shall pray for you. I have asked four people to do the same, and each of them was…"

"…killed?"

"Yes."

"But *why* does he kill people?"

"Fresh human liver fetches a very high price. They say that it cures almost any illness."

With that, she slipped quietly away.

An hour later there was a violent knocking at the door.

"Breakfast!" the man shouted. I checked my pockets. Making sure I had enough money for my journey back to Tokyo, I wrapped the rest in a piece of paper and handed it to the man as I came out of the shed.

"There's twelve or thirteen yen there. Please take it. I am very grateful to you for allowing me to stay."

The man took it without comment, as though it was his due.

"The wife's made some *mochi*," he said. "There's nothing better than a stomach full of *mochi* to keep you going through the snow."

I sat down at the edge of the hearth and was given my breakfast straightaway – *mochi* rice cake in walnut and fern soup. In other circumstances it would have seemed a fine meal, but I was in no state to enjoy it now.

I desperately tried to forestall any offer from the man to act as guide on my way to the village. I hinted repeatedly that I could find my own way.

"No chance of getting lost today!" I said. "Last night was tough, but today will be fine… I did a lot of skiing in my university days, so I'm used to mountain paths, you know… I go along that path in front of the house straight down to the village. Couldn't be easier!"

"That was delicious!" I said finally, putting down my chopsticks and rising to my feet. "Thank you very much for everything you have done!" By this time I was on the earthen floor putting on my shoes. "Right," I muttered vaguely and rushed out of the door.

The man had not yet spoken. It looked as though I was going to get away. I ran through the deep snow across the garden and out onto the path. Then I heard the man's voice behind me.

"What's the rush?"

I felt as though an icicle had been put down my back. I shivered.

"It's not going to snow this morning," he said. "You should go slowly."

I turned around to see the man spring lightly off the veranda and put on his straw snow-boots. I whistled in a show of courage and pretended to examine the sky.

"You're right," I said. "The weather looks fine. I'll take it easy."

The man came out onto the path.

"Yes," he said. "You do that! But you'll still get lost in the snow – there are no signs on the path. I'll come down with you to the village."

It was as if a chasm had opened up in the path and I'd fallen straight in.

"N-no," I said. "I'll be fine."

"I've got one or two things to do in the village," he said, "so I'll come down with you. It's no trouble."

"Really, I'll be all right."

"You're a strange bastard!" he growled. "It's not often I try to be kind – once in three years maybe, more like once in five. And what happens? You throw it back in my face!"

He grabbed my coat lapels with tremendous force and twisted them upwards in his fists. Buttons flew through the air. Beyond him I could see the woman standing on the veranda. She was looking sadly towards us, slowly shaking her head. Her expression seemed to say: "Do as my husband says, and escape later!"

"Of course," I said to the man. "I would be extremely grateful if you were to show me the way. I hesitated to accept your offer simply because I did not want to trouble you."

The man pushed me away and shouted for Shiro. So his dog was coming too. Even if I could get away from the man, I didn't stand a chance of escaping the dog. It would catch me up before I'd run thirty metres.

"Let's go!" said the man.

I followed like a convict on the way to the gallows. Behind me came the dog, growling fiercely as if to say: "One false move and I bite!"

The path zig-zagged down the mountain through forest – it was hardly surprising I'd lost my way the night before. When we came out of the forest, there was a cliff on one side of the path, and at the bottom of the cliff was another path, running in parallel. As we walked on, the height of the cliff lessened, and the two paths grew closer. At last I saw a *jizo* statue. Beyond that we came to some thick bamboo grass covered in snow.

"Here we are!" I thought.

I kept walking, but now in a very awkward manner.

"What's the matter with you?" said the man.

"My bladder's full," I said, scratching my head. "May I..."

"Well, all right," said the man. "I'll join you!"

It looked like he was going to take a long time relieving himself, and the dog too had its leg raised against a tree.

"Now's my chance!" I thought.

I threw myself onto the bamboo grass. With the snow hastening my descent, I slid straight down onto the lower path. From there I saw the temple gate, just as the woman had said. I started running towards it.

The man was yelling on the path above, his equipment still in full flow. The dog barked wildly as it saw its master's agitation. But it was not long before the man sorted himself out and when I had run just fifty metres I heard him shout:

"Shiro! After him!"

My mind was racing, but my legs were slow. By the time I reached the temple gate, the dog was just thirty metres behind me. To my dismay the gate was shut. There were two large fittings on the gate, side by side, the shape of upturned bowls. I grabbed them and shook them, rattling the gate.

"Open up! Help!" I was almost screaming.

From inside the gate I heard the shriek of a young woman.

"Ahhh!"

My heart froze. It was the voice of my wife – my wife, who I thought was at that moment lying dangerously ill in Tokyo.

The snarling dog leapt towards me. As I wondered how on earth my wife could be at this mountain temple, I felt the dog's sharp claws in my back. I clutched ever harder at the bowl-shaped fittings on the gate. Again I heard my wife scream from inside.'

Inubuse suddenly stopped. He glanced at me mischievously.

'Hearing my wife scream, I woke with a start. It was a dream. I realised that the bowl shaped fittings were in fact my wife's breasts. I had grabbed and shaken them in my sleep and she had screamed. The claws in my back were my wife's nails…'

And then I saw for the first time that Inubuse had completely fooled me.

'So it was all a dream, from the start?'

'Yes.'

'That's ridiculous!'

'You've no right to be cross. You could have known it wasn't true. It's hardly likely that an orchestra would have visited an out-of-the-way place like this in the 1920s, is it? That was a typical story from this area. I used the trumpet as the starting point this time – you can use a different prop and end up with a slightly different story. That's the beauty of it. I can tell you plenty of stories like that one if you like.'

I leant over to the mouth of the cave and looked out. The sleet had turned to snow. I stood up.

'Next time, please will you tell me the secret of your trumpet and why you came to live in the mountains?'

Inubuse stretched himself out on the wooden floor.

'Certainly,' he said. 'Please come again.'

He waved to me as I walked away.

川上の家
House up the River

After that first autumn, my work at the sanatorium was based in the accounts office. Inubuse still always began to play his trumpet at twelve noon. That was the start of my lunch hour, so the trumpet signalled redemption – release, for a while, from the drudgery of calculating nurses' pay and doctors' travel allowances. As soon as the faint notes penetrated the office I would pick up my lunch and rush outside. A narrow mountain pathway led from the sanatorium along the stream up to the old man's cave. If I hurried I could be there in five minutes. By the time I arrived he had always stopped playing and would be making tea. Taking hot water from a kettle suspended over the hearth, he brewed the tea in a small earthenware pot and then poured it into the chipped cups. He would call out to me as I peered in at the entrance.

'Tea's ready, young man. Will you have a cup?'

I would stoop through the cave entrance, sit down at the hearth, take a sip of tea, and open my lunch. After a while, the old man would start, in a very quiet voice, to tell old tales of the surrounding country – the area around Tono and Kamaishi. And as he talked I would eat my lunch. He told me how the *kappa* in the region had red faces, not blue as elsewhere. He told me how the local monkeys rubbed themselves with pine resin and sand to harden their coats and repel hunters' bullets. He told me never to forget to take *mochi* rice cake when going into the mountains. *Mochi* was a great favourite with Mountain Men and would never fail to get these seven-foot giants on to your side. They would be so grateful they would protect you from the wolves, and from the tricks and traps of foxes and badgers. They would show you what path to take; and when there was no path, they would make one for you.

In fact, though, I was more interested in Inubuse himself. He had told me that as a young man he had been in an orchestra in Tokyo. But I knew nothing else about him – where he was born, his upbringing, how he came to be living in a place like this.

One spring day, when I had been visiting him for some time, I asked him, as I had on several previous occasions, where he was born. I had never had a proper answer before. He had always looked away in silence, or hurriedly changed the subject, or angrily said: 'What does it matter?' That day, however, he seemed in unusually good spirits. I expect this was because of the season – everybody in the north feels happy when the warm dark earth shows its face from under the snow. And perhaps he was beginning to feel a slight affection for the young man who came to his cave each lunch-time and listened in silence to his stories. Anyway, for the first time he actually answered my question.

'I was born near here, in Hashino,' he said.

Hashino is a village north of the sanatorium, deep in the mountains, across Katsushi River and over Mount Senban. As the crow flies it is about fifteen kilometres, but the paths are steep and winding, so even a good walker would take a whole day to get there. I had been there once myself – chasing up payment for a sanatorium bill – and I had been surprised at how large the village was.

'I expected just five or six houses,' I had said to the innkeeper when I arrived. 'But there's a proper street – almost like a country town.'

'There's an iron mine just outside the village,' he said. 'That's why it's prosperous.'

During the night I heard animals screeching on the mountainside behind the inn.

'The monkeys were noisy last night,' I said to the innkeeper the next morning.

He waved his hand in front of his face dismissively.

'They're not monkeys,' he said. 'They're *kappa*. They move from the river to the mountains when the season changes. When they're on the move they screech like monkeys.'

'Do you really think they are *kappa*?' I asked. 'Have you seen any?'

'They never show themselves to humans in their true form. But they're *kappa* right enough. Screeching means the *kappa* are on the move. That's what we say round here.'

He had been very obstinate about it. According to him, there were several thousand *kappa* in the Hashino River, but when in water they were translucent, like jellyfish. In fact they couldn't be seen with human eyes at all. Once they were out of the river they took the form of children or travellers. In the mountains they appeared as monkeys or pheasants. They could change size as well as appearance – a thousand *kappa* could hide in the puddle of a horse's hoof print.

'But,' he said, eyeing me suspiciously, 'more often than not *kappa* appear as travellers. That's what we say round here.'

'What do you mean?' I said. 'I'm a human being! I work at the National Sanatorium at Kamaishi!' I stormed angrily out of the inn.

Hashino was a very strange place.

'My father was employed by the iron mine as a seam-searcher,' Inubuse began. 'His job was to search the mountains for iron deposits that could be mined.' He sipped his tea slowly, as if it were *sake*. 'My father was always walking in the mountains, and only came home two or three times a month. Our house was a lonely and frightening place. When the wind howled in the mountains, or heavy rains made the river roar, we couldn't sleep at all.

My mother said that if my father found just one seam he would get a five-hundred yen reward. Five hundred yen was a lot of money in those days. She said they would use it to start a business in town, and that we would never have to spend another lonely night in the house. As a little boy I always prayed that my father would find that iron seam. But it always eluded him. He got the job in Hashino two years before I was born. He spent the next twelve years, until the incident, walking through the mountains between Tono and Kamaishi: Mount Iwakura, Mount Senban, Odake, Obiraki-yama Mount Gorosaku, Mount Rokkoushi – but he didn't come across a single seam.'

Inubuse's voice suddenly broke off. I stopped eating and looked at him. He was staring out towards the mountains – at the bright patches of colour on the hillside. The wild cherry trees were beginning to flower. He gazed at them sadly for a while. Then he shook his head and continued with his story.

'It was spring. I was in the third year at Hashino Elementary School and my brother, Ryokichi, was in the first year. There are a lot of cherry trees in Hashino and our route to school took us along a beautiful row of them on the embankment above the river. My brother and I were walking to school one day when, to our surprise, we saw a boy ahead of us. He looked as though he was on his way to school too. I say "to our surprise" because just a few moments earlier there had been nobody there. He must have been under a tree, or perhaps he had climbed up from the river. He wore a short striped kimono and on his feet were new straw sandals. The sandals were sopping wet and left dark wet footprints on the dry embankment. Normally you would expect straw sandals to dry out a little after ten paces or so, but strangely the footprints remained very wet however far he walked.

"He's come up from the river," I thought. "He must have been fishing."

Hashino Elementary School had only about seventy pupils, so of course we knew everyone's face – in fact, we could identify anybody at the school from just a yell, or a glimpse of their back. The figure in front of us was not familiar at all.

"Who's that?" we muttered to each other as we walked on.

Suddenly he turned around. He had an extraordinary face. For one thing it was red, as if he had been rubbing red soil into his skin. And it was wrinkled, even though he was just a child. And he had large eyes completely out of proportion to the rest of his face. He reminded me of a monkey – in fact, he looked exactly like one. His mouth protruded, as if it had been pinched and pulled forward. It was like the face of a gargoyle at the village shrine. Ryokichi and I looked at each other and sniggered. The boy scratched his head and smiled bashfully. As he did so his thin lips seemed to crack open as far as his ears. I blinked in astonishment and looked again, but by then his lips were closed. The boy bowed quickly and hurried on along the embankment.

With just seventy or so pupils, the school was divided into two groups. Year One to Year Three formed one group and Year Four to Year Six the other. That morning, when the bell rang, the teacher came into our classroom accompanied by a boy.

"You have a new classmate," the teacher said. "This is Kotaro Kawabe. He comes from Akashiba School, upriver. He is a third-year, so I want you other third-years to look after him."

It was, of course, the boy from the embankment. He again smiled bashfully as the teacher introduced him. Ryokichi and I stared at his mouth, but nothing unusual happened this time. It must have been an illusion, I thought in relief. People's mouths don't open like that – not unless they're cats in disguise.

Kotaro was given the desk next to mine. He seemed nice – very quiet. Whatever I said to him, he would simply smile in silence. When I said "Good morning" he would smile; when I said "Goodbye" he would smile again. At first I thought he might be dumb. Sometimes, though, he was asked to read aloud in class. He seemed to know so few characters that I wondered what he had been taught up in Akashiba. And he had a terribly high-pitched voice. When he started to read, I could just about manage to catch his words, but his pitch grew higher and higher as he continued and after a while he would sound like a screeching monkey. By that time I had no idea which sentence he was reading.

When it came to arithmetic, he was worse than my brother in the first year. The teacher once asked him:

"What do you get if you divide nine *manju* cakes among three brothers?"

Kotaro thought long and hard and then said:

"A quarrel."

The class roared with laughter. After that the teacher hardly ever asked Kotaro to answer a question again. He realised that he would never get a proper answer.

While Kotaro was hopeless at schoolwork, he excelled at anything physical. In gymnastics, which the whole school did together, he was as good as any of the pupils in Year Six. He was particularly skilful on the horizontal bar, performing movements that even the teacher couldn't manage. Although he was small he was very strong, and he wrestled with the teacher on equal terms.

When it was time to clean the classroom and the toilets at the end of each day, he immediately set to work with a broom and cloth, and did not stop until everything was finished. The areas that Kotaro cleaned stood out from the rest – the surfaces really shone, and there wasn't a speck of dust on the floor.

The time he really made a name for himself was when we went picking ferns. In the Hashino area, late May to early June is fern season. There were no lessons and pupils were sent out to the mountains to gather ferns. The ferns were then dried, bundled, loaded onto horses, and taken by the school janitor down to the coast at Kamaishi and Ozuchi, where they were sold to greengrocers. The money was spent on schoolbooks and winter fuel. Every day Kotaro gathered two or three times as many ferns as anybody else in the school. And he also brought back mountain-lily roots. Lily roots boiled with sugar are a great delicacy around here, and can be sold for very high prices in the towns. The roots lie deep in the earth, so they are normally too difficult for children to extract. But Kotaro pulled up the root of every lily he saw. Everybody was amazed at how hard he worked.'

Inubuse paused, and gulping down the rest of his tea, took off his quilted jacket – the story seemed to be warming him up.

'A mysterious child coming to a village school,' I said. 'It sounds like one of Kenji Miyazawa's stories. The child makes friends with everyone and then suddenly goes off to another school. Is that what's going to happen?'

'I'd rather you didn't make silly remarks,' Inubuse said sharply, stroking his grizzled beard. 'You're thinking of "Matasaburo the Wind Imp." I guarantee this story is very different.'

'How is it different?'

'It's sadder. More painful.'

The old man hunched his back, so that he looked smaller.

'Kotaro and I soon became friends,' he said. 'It would have been odd if we hadn't. We were in the same year, we sat next to each other, and, because we both lived upriver, we walked to and from school together. Every morning Kotaro would come to our house half an hour before Ryokichi and I normally set off. Always smiling, he would watch us get ready. On the way back from school, he would come into the house for an hour before carrying on to his own home. If he grew tired of playing, he would go out to the back of the house and chop wood – nobody asked him to.

My mother was very fond of him. If Ryokichi or I were slow doing some chores, she would say: "You should be more like Kotaro!"

"What does your father do, Kotaro?" my mother asked one day. She had brought us a snack while we were looking at some picture books in the main room.

"He's dead," said Kotaro in his high-pitched voice.

"Oh, I'm sorry," she said. "But you have a mother, don't you?"

"Yes, but she's ill."

"Oh dear! Do you have brothers and sisters?"

"No."

My mother grew anxious.

"Are you sure your mother is all right alone? I think you had better go home to look after her."

"It's okay," said Kotaro. "She'll be better soon."

As he spoke, he continued to leaf through a picture book. He sounded very confident.

My mother continued with her questions.

"What sort of illness does she have?"

"I don't know. But she'll be better once she gets her medicine."

"What medicine?"

Kotaro fell silent. His red face was suddenly pale. Just then a visitor arrived so we didn't find out what medicine it was. My mother left the room and the conversation ended. I remember Kotaro breathing a sigh of relief.

Some time later, one drizzling afternoon in the middle of the rainy season, Kotaro and I were playing in the house as usual – rummaging through the pile of picture books, or maybe playing checkers on a grid we had drawn on the back of an exercise book. My brother Ryokichi came into the room holding a glass.

"Ko-chan," he said to Kotaro. "Shall I show you some magic?" He put the glass on the table and covered it with a handkerchief.

"Ladies and gentlemen, prepare to be amazed! Before your very eyes in this empty glass a flower will bloom. Abracadabra!"

Having stumbled through this little speech, Ryoikichi whipped the handkerchief off the glass. Inside was a small red artificial flower. The glass was a present from my father who had come home recently. He had bought it by the coast on his way back from the mountains. It was a trick glass, of course, but Kotaro stared at the flower open-mouthed.

"My turn now!" I said, taking the handkerchief from Ryokichi. I stretched it out and waved it in the air in front of Kotaro.

"Ladies and gentlemen," I began. "Behold this single solitary handkerchief!"

I placed it on the table and spread my bare palms in front of Kotaro's eyes.

"Witness, if you will! My left hand is empty! My right hand is empty!"

I picked up the handkerchief again, rubbed it between my hands and concealed it in my left fist.

"And now – mystery of mysteries! This handkerchief will have a child! Hey presto!"

The handkerchief was also a present from my father. The trick was simple – the handkerchief had a pocket embroidered on its edge, and this pocket contained a smaller handkerchief. All you had to do was to distract people's attention with words as you pulled the small handkerchief out. When I waved the two handkerchiefs in the air, Kotaro let out a low animal-like growl.

"Now it's your turn, Ko-chan!" shouted Ryokichi. "We've both shown you some magic – now you do some!"

Kotaro was silent. His red face had turned pale, just as when my mother asked him about the medicine.

"It doesn't matter what! Just do something!" Ryokichi insisted.

Kotaro swallowed hard, and nodded.

"You've both done magic, so I must as well."

He stretched his hand towards me.

"Takichi, lend me your handkerchief."

"Here you are," I said. "What are you are going to do?"

"I'm going to produce something from under the handkerchief – anything that Ryo-chan wants."

"Liar!" said Ryokichi. "You can't do that!"

"But I must."

Kotaro waved the handkerchief in the air just as I had done.

"Ryo-chan, you produced a flower. And Takichi, you produced a baby handkerchief. I must produce something."

"Okay then, a dog! Produce a dog!" said Ryokichi, skipping around Kotaro. "Make it a shiba! A shiba puppy!"

Kotaro spread the handkerchief out on the table. Then, holding his right palm over the handkerchief, he uttered a kind of spell.

The handkerchief started to move and swell. From beneath came a sound, like the whimpering of a puppy. Suddenly the handkerchief rose up into the air, and there, on the table, was a newborn shiba puppy struggling clumsily to its feet, its eyes still closed.

Ryokichi gasped and clutched onto me. I gripped him tight in turn, glad to have someone to hold on to.

Kotaro was trembling. Eventually he picked up the handkerchief and spread it over the puppy. The puppy immediately disappeared and the handkerchief again lay flat on the table. Kotaro picked it up and wiped the sweat from his forehead.

"Well," he said. "You got your shiba puppy, didn't you?"

"That was amazing! A really great bit of magic! What's the dodge?" I asked.

Kotaro looked blank.

"The dodge…?" he said.

"Yes," I said. "What was the trick?"

"The trick?"

I showed Kotaro how Ryokichi had produced the flower, and how I had produced the little handkerchief.

"That's what we did. What did you do?"

We each took one of Kotaro's hands and begged him to tell us. He shook our hands away with tremendous strength.

"You were both cheating! But I… I…"

He began to sob. Rising to his feet as lightly as the handkerchief had risen into the air, he went straight out into the drizzling rain.'

Inubuse poured some more tea into his cup and sipped it, staring at me intently.

'Is that it?' I said. 'Is that the end of the story?'

'Calm yourself!' he said. 'That's just the start.'

He slowly finished his tea, and then resumed his story.

'The next day – Sunday, it must have been – I went down to the river immediately after breakfast and started walking upstream. After his mysterious magic trick Kotaro had rushed out of the house barefoot, leaving his school things inside and his straw sandals at the front door. I decided to take them to his house. Strangely, although we were very good friends, I had never been to his house. I had often asked him if I could visit, but he always discouraged me. He said his mother would get cross if we spoke loudly. He said it would be boring, because they didn't have any toys or books. He said the house was in the middle of nowhere – it would be all right getting there because we would be together, but it would be frightening for me on the way back.

"Okay," I had once said. "You don't have to take me to your house, but at least tell me about it."

Kotaro had reluctantly described where the house was:

"It's straight upriver – about half an hour. On the right there's a mill and beside the mill there's a thatched house. That's where I live."

With this description in mind, I walked upriver. Thirty minutes went by, an hour – but I saw no mill. The river was narrowing, the mountains closing in on either side. There was less and less space in which to walk beside the water. It started to drizzle, a white fog rolling down the mountains on either side. I could no longer see clearly around me. I walked on until eventually there was no shore left. I wanted to climb up onto the bank, but I could not see any way up from the riverbed. The harsh cry of an unfamiliar bird pierced the fog above me. I started to shiver. I must have been walking for two hours. Why hadn't I come across the mill? Had I missed it? Could I really have missed something as large as a mill? Ko-chan must have been lying – there was no other explanation. His house must be somewhere else. I decided to go home.

Turning to face downriver, I shuddered. Two white water snakes, each over six feet long, were swimming slowly across the river. People say that water snakes do no harm to humans, but even if that is true they are an unpleasant sight. I decided to wait, thinking that they would soon disappear; but they stopped in a shallow near the river's edge, raised their necks, and looked towards me. Their eyes were cold, cruel, dead-men's eyes. I was terrified. I began to sob with fear. Just then I heard a sound from upriver… *creak-creak*… the noise of the shaft of a millwheel. I turned and tried to make out where the noise came from. Gradually, on the right bank upstream, the fog abated. I could see a large millwheel turning slowly. I took off my straw sandals and, holding them in my hand, stepped into the fast-flowing river. Taking the shallowest route, I waded towards the mill.

Beside the mill was a large thatched house – just as Kotaro had said. I climbed up onto the bank beside the mill and stood in the front garden of the house. My heart was pounding. In a faltering voice I called Kotaro's name, but there was no reply. I looked around me and listened. There was no sign of anyone.

I walked nervously towards the house. Everything was closed – except one storm shutter. I peered in. It was eerily dark inside. I sat down at the opening. Kotaro had told the truth after all – here was the house next to the mill. But how strange that he had said it was half an hour away! It would take at least an hour and a half to walk here, even if one was used to the journey. Why would he have lied about that? I looked around at the mountains, dimly visible through the drizzling rain.

"I'll wait for Kotaro to come home," I thought.

Just at that moment, I heard a hoarse, melancholy voice from inside the house.

"Kotaro! Are you back?"

I was very surprised and, turning towards the house, I looked again through the open storm shutter. As my eyes grew accustomed to the darkness, I made out the figure of an old woman lying on a futon, trying desperately to get up. That must be Kotaro's sick mother, I thought. She lifted her arm and beckoned to me. It looked like a withered branch.

"I… I'm not Kotaro," I stuttered, passing through the open shutter. "I'm his friend Takichi Inubuse."

But the old woman seemed convinced that I was Kotaro and continued to beckon me. I moved across the room to where she lay. When I saw her face I all but screamed. It was dry and shrivelled, like that of an old monkey. It was red, speckled with black, and fretted with wrinkles. Her eyes, as large as Kotaro's, were clouded white. She reached out and clasped my hand. I looked down and saw webbing between her fingers. Horrified, I tried to pull my hand away. But she drew it towards her with a strength I would not have believed possible in a sick old woman.

"Kotaro," she groaned. "I shall die..."

The characteristic sour smell of a bedridden patient was combined with a raw, pungent stench of flesh.

"Please, Kotaro! Give me some liver! I'll get better if I have some liver..."

She gripped my hand tight. Her skin was colder than a mountain stream. Why would she want liver? Liver isn't a medicine! My head pounded with fear.

"Takichi! What are you doing here?"

Kotaro had appeared on the veranda outside. What a relief! I felt like a traveller who spies a welcoming lantern on a dark night. With all my strength I shook my hand free of the old woman's clutch and went over to him.

"You left your things at our house yesterday," I said. "I've brought them over for you."

He didn't smile.

"Has she said anything?" he asked sternly. I shook my head. I felt he might murder me if I told him about the liver.

"Did you see her hands?"

I shook my head again.

"Are you telling the truth?" He stared into my eyes. His look seemed to pierce deep down inside me. But I resolved to keep lying.

"Yes," I said.

"Well, all right." His voice was suddenly cheerful and high-pitched. "I'll walk with you part of the way back."

He signalled me to come outside.

On the way home, the two white snakes were no longer to be seen. The fog had disappeared, the drizzle had stopped, and the midday sun blazed down on the river shore. A powerful smell emanated from the thick-growing mugwort. It seemed that the rainy season had come to an end.

The season had indeed changed. It was now summer in Hashino, and we began to swim in the river.

A week after my visit to Kotaro's house, my brother drowned. Ryokichi and I had been playing all morning in a river pool when Kotaro came running down towards us.

"Can I join in?" he said.

"Of course!" we said.

We were delighted, because we knew that he would show us some of his dives. I said earlier that he was a marvellous gymnast; his diving was amazing too. He would climb high up and do back-flips from places that anybody else – even the best swimmers and the bravest miners – would hesitate to dive from at all. It was a wonderful sight – it made you feel good just to watch him.

"Will you do some dives?" Ryokichi asked Kotaro as the three of us splashed and wrestled in the water.

"Okay," nodded Kotaro, smiling. "But you must show me your diving as well, Ryo-chan."

"But I can only dive from there," said Ryokichi, pointing to a rock about three feet above the surface.

"That's all right.. Have a go!"

Ryokichi clambered up onto the rock and dived in with a splash. He didn't come up again.

Kotaro was the first to get upset.

"That's strange," he said. "He's been down there over a minute."

I felt my face grow pale. Ryokichi was only seven. He surely couldn't stay under water that long with lungs as small as his. Kotaro and I dived down after him. We searched the bed of the river pool time and again, but he wasn't there.

"He's not here!" I cried. Some children playing nearby heard me. They rushed about in confusion until one of them found an adult. Over the next three days every man and woman in the village joined the search for Ryokichi, but they couldn't find him.

An official from the mine hurried to find my father, who was searching for iron seams deep in the mountains. Apparently when they found him he was laughing out loud, all on his own. At around noon that Sunday – just at the time when Ryokichi was drowned – he had found a large seam of iron. It was a very strange coincidence.

Ryokichi's bloated body was eventually found a week later, downriver at a place called Unosumai. His bowels and liver had been removed, skilfully extracted through his anus.'

Inubuse stopped talking. He sat motionless for a while, his eyes tight shut.

'It was Kotaro that did it, wasn't it?' I said. 'He was a *kappa*, wasn't he? He took your brother's bowels and liver to make his mother better, didn't her? That's it, isn't it?'

The old man did not respond. His eyes remained tight shut.

'He was a *kappa*, wasn't he? He pretended to be human and he went to school because he wanted human organs. Your father finding the iron seam was the *kappa*'s way of making amends.'

'Maybe so,' said Inubuse. 'But then again, maybe not.'

He tipped the teapot spout over his cup. There was none left. He clicked his tongue quietly and put the pot down on the edge of the hearth.

'It may have all been coincidence. The puppy under the handkerchief may really have been a trick. His mother's webbed fingers may have been an illusion. Perhaps she didn't say "liver" at all.'

'But then how do you explain the fact that your brother's liver and bowels were missing?'

'Perhaps they were eaten by fish.'

'That's not very likely.'

'Anyway, my father got his reward for finding the iron seam and using that money the family moved to Tokyo and set up a shop. It was after we got to Tokyo that I began to learn the trumpet.'

'What happened to Kotaro?

'He died a month later.'

The old man pressed a piece of cigarette into the bowl of his pipe.

'In fact,' he said, 'there was a rumour in Hashino that my brother had been killed by a *kappa*. So he was given a black funeral.'

'What's a black funeral?'

'A funeral where there are no lights and nothing white at all – not even cloths or paper. People here say that if you hold a black funeral, the *kappa* that caused the death will gradually lose its sight and strength, and then die. So they held a black funeral for Ryokichi. After that Kotaro developed a strange illness, wasted away, and died.'

'That proves it!' I said. 'He was a *kappa*!'

I stood up and put my head out of the cave entrance. It was almost the end of my lunch hour.

'Kotaro was a *kappa* and his death was a punishment!' I said.

Again Inubuse said nothing. He lit the cigarette in his pipe, and inhaled deeply.

雉子娘
Pheasant Girl

'This area has been hit by famine many times over the years,' said Inubuse as soon as I stepped into the cave. 'Today I'm going to tell you a story that relates to the famine of 1931.'

It was early May and I was visiting Inubuse as usual on my lunch break. His manner suggested that I had kept him waiting.

'Things were so desperate that throughout the district the village offices displayed notices saying: "Those wishing to sell their daughters should consult inside."'

I sat down opposite Inubuse on the near side of the hearth. Azaleas were in full flower on the mountains outside. Their powerful bittersweet smell pervaded the cave.

The old man's face was redder than usual. I wondered why. It wasn't heat from the hearth – even deep in the Tohoku mountains, May is warm enough not to have a fire. Nor was it because of drink – at least, there was no smell of alcohol.

He broke a cigarette into three pieces, put one in his pipe, lit it with a match, and inhaled deeply. He was looking past me, through the mouth of the cave. His impatience was gone and he was now deep in thought. I turned and followed his gaze. He seemed to be looking at the profusion of brick-coloured azaleas on the mountainside opposite. It was almost as if the colour in his face was a reflection of those flowers.

'As I told you before,' he said, 'when I was a child my family lived in the village of Hashino.'

He put the second piece of cigarette into his pipe, and then slowly settled his gaze on me.

'My memories of Hashino are not happy. My little brother died a strange death in the river there. My father was often away from home – he was an engineer at the Kamaishi Mine and went for long trips into the mountains looking for iron deposits. When I was about twelve, he found an iron seam and the mining company gave him a reward of five hundred yen. It was a lot of money in those days. My parents talked incessantly about how it might be used. My mother didn't like Hashino any more than I did and saw the money as a means of escape. She wanted my father to give up his job straightaway so that we could move to Tokyo. My father would have preferred to carry on searching for new iron deposits, but he grew weary of trying to convince my mother, and in the end agreed to move to the capital. This sent my mother into a delirium of happiness.

"We're going to Tokyo! We're going to live in Tokyo!" she cried, hugging me as I was studying at my desk.

She didn't normally behave like that – she was basically an old-fashioned woman who didn't allow her emotions to show. I was very surprised and embarrassed. It may be fine for a little child, but it's very uncomfortable for a boy of eleven or twelve to be treated like that by his mother.'

I had brought two large jam rolls with me to the cave. I took them out of their paper bag and placed one in front of Inubuse. I used to buy rolls at the sanatorium in the morning and looked forward to sharing them with Inubuse at lunchtime. He snuffed out his pipe on the edge of the hearth and picked up the roll. Tearing off scraps of bread, he tossed them one at a time into his mouth. I reached over to the water jar, filled a cup and placed that in front him too. He gulped it down in one.

'But things didn't go well in Tokyo,' he said.

'Why?' I asked, gripping my roll tightly in both hands and pulling away a hunk with my teeth – the sanatorium's rolls were baked hard and there was quite a knack to biting into them.

'Supplementing the five-hundred-yen reward with a thousand-yen loan from his family, my father started an ironmongery business in the East Ryogoku area of Tokyo. Things were fine at first, but the business couldn't cope with the depression of the 1920s. In the end there was nothing for it but to abandon the business and run off from the creditors. A lot of people did the same thing at that time.'

'Where did you go?'

'It was only my father who went…'

'But he must have let you know secretly where he was so that you could join him…'

'He didn't even tell my mother he was going. He had a prostitute with him, apparently. We heard no more about him after that.'

'What happened to your mother?'

'She was hounded day and night by the creditors. She never slept for worry, and six months later she died.'

'Hold on!' I said. 'You told me that your father borrowed a thousand yen from his family when you went to Tokyo. They must have been pretty rich to come up with a thousand yen in those days. Why didn't your mother ask them for help?'

Inubuse looked deep into my eyes and shook his head.

'Nobody is colder in a crisis than relatives. My father's family were major landowners, well-known in this area, with fifty tenant farmers. But when his business failed they were more ruthless than anyone in trying to get their capital back. They sent thugs round in the end. It's no exaggeration to say the family's bully-boy tactics destroyed my mother's health.'

'And what were *you* doing at that time?'

'I was at high school. I was more interested in music than study and I spent all my time playing the trumpet.'

Inubuse turned and glanced at the instrument hanging from a nail at the back of the cave.

'I hoped one day to make my living from the trumpet. But with my father's disappearance, my mother's death and the house being sold to pay off the debts, I had to do more than just practise my instrument. I gave up school and tried working for my living. But joblessness was a real problem in Tokyo – nearly two hundred thousand men were out of work. "I went to university, but…" had become a kind of catchphrase. So there wasn't much going for a youngster who'd just dropped out of high school. There were a dozen employment offices in Tokyo, but to have a hope of a day's work you had to be queuing outside the office by two or three in the morning. And any work you got was sheer exploitation. One time I painted patterns on *fusuma* screens. It was simple work – putting a stencil of leaves and flowers on the white paper and rubbing with a brush, but the rate of pay was only two sen per hundred screens. And after you'd had one bit of work, you had to wait ten or fifteen days before they'd give you anything else. It almost destroyed me. I ended up spending three whole days lying on a bench in Asakusa Park. I was well on my way to joining Tokyo's five-thousand-strong army of vagrants.'

'So what did you do?'

'On my fourth day in Asakusa I made up my mind to go to my father's family. I hated them for what they'd done to my mother, and I expected no kindness. But I had managed to pay off the loan by selling the house in Ryogoku and I thought the head of the family might at least agree to put me up in the corner of a barn. He was my uncle, after all. So I went to a second-hand instrument store in Ueno, sold my beloved trumpet, and with the proceeds bought a train ticket north. It was the summer of 1931.'

Inubuse bit at his roll in silence for a while, before a thought seemed to come to him.

'Do you know the area around Kuro Wood,' he said, 'on the road to the sanatorium?'

The sanatorium was about twelve kilometres from where I lived in Kamaishi, and about half that distance was through the mountains. Where the road flattened out, there was a large dark wood, known as Kuro Wood, or Black Wood. It was a very eerie place. It was a full kilometre from the road, but if I was late going home I could always hear its trees rustling, even on a windless night. Between the road and the wood was a river about five metres wide. It was fast-flowing and I always heard the sound of the water as I walked along the road. When night fell it would suddenly seem like a human voice – a young woman whispering and sobbing.

'The river there is called Kiji River, or Pheasant River,' Inubuse said. 'The family house was between the river and Kuro Wood. My uncle was a big landowner and the house was a grand one. It had a fine gateway to the east, but there was no wall around the property – the estate was too large for that. The land reached as far as where we are now. Most of it was rented out to the fifty tenant farmers, but some was retained to supply food to the household. Five labourers were employed to work on this land, and they lived in huts dotted around the fields. Each of the huts was divided into a living area and an area for stabling and storage. And there amongst the huts stood the family house. The contrast was vast. The house and huts were as different as snow and mud, a lord's castle and beggars' hovels.

The house had a fine thatch, two-foot thick. Its timber was all cypress. Inside the back entrance was an earthen floor spacious enough to accommodate one or even two ordinary houses. On the left was a vast kitchen, with a hearth cut into the floor. The ceiling, beams and pillars were black from the smoke of the hearth. The dark floor was polished like a mirror. To the right, I think, were the stables. Beautifully groomed black and chestnut horses snorted an alarm as I came into the house. The earthen floor was thirty paces long. About two thirds of the way across stood a huge cauldron on a clay base. The cauldron was used to cook rice for the whole household – five gallons each morning and evening. When I reached the end of the earthen floor I took off my shoes and stepped up into a long corridor stretching twenty metres ahead. On the right was a garden and on the left was a series of rooms: the tea ceremony room, the altar room, the middle reception room, and the upper reception room. I did not know it at the time but further over were three sleeping rooms, a store room and the blind-men's room.'

I was trying hard to build a picture of the house in my mind as Inubuse spoke – but I had no idea what a blind-men's room could be.

'What's that?' I asked

Inubuse explained.

'In the old days, when a landowner of the district had a party, he would always employ blind entertainers. They would play the *biwa*, tell stories, perform comic dances, and sometimes give massages. The blind-men's room was where they waited and slept.'

'I walked along the corridor,' Inubuse continued, 'and in the tea ceremony room sat a thin-faced man of about sixty, smoking. As soon as I saw him I guessed he was my uncle, the head of the family.'

'Had you never seen him before?' I asked.

Inubuse shook his head.

'My father had argued with the family. He had refused to accept the marriage they proposed for him, and chose his own wife instead. And as a result he was virtually disowned. After that, except in very special circumstances, he never went near them. So naturally I had never visited them. Of course, when they wanted to collect the debt, they sent servants and thugs rather than coming themselves. So this was the first time I had seen my uncle.

'The man looked at my face for a while,' continued Inubuse, 'and soon noticed a resemblance to his younger brother.

"You're the Hashino boy, aren't you?" he said sourly.

Hashino, of course, was the name of the village where my father had lived.

"Why have you come here?"

There was a shade of caution in his face. He must have thought I was going to take him to task for his shameful treatment of my mother.

I bowed.

"Please allow me to stay here for a time," I said. "It is impossible for me to live in Tokyo."

He sneered.

"We're in no position to have hangers-on, relative or no relative."

I found out later that two years of bad harvests had made life very difficult for landowners as well as tenant farmers.

The landowners' rents were fixed at half the rice the tenants grew. So rents went down when harvests were poor. And to make matters worse, the price of rice had fallen because of the depression. So the landowners' income had inevitably shrunk. And from this income, they had to pay taxes. So while of course they didn't suffer the same miseries as the tenant farmers, things were not at all easy for them. Unlike today, the central government did not make any payments to rural districts, so local finances had to be covered entirely by local taxes. Some rich landowners moved to towns in order to avoid the high taxes. This left the remaining landowners having to pay even more. But the family at Kuro Wood was too long-established to abscond. They were too well-known, their lands were too large – it would have been altogether too shameful. As a result the family found themselves having to pay one third of the local taxes.

At the time I didn't know any of this, but it wouldn't have made any difference. I had no option but to beg my uncle to take me in. I bowed down, my face on the floor.

"I'll work in the fields," I said. "I'll do anything. Please just feed me! Please let me stay!"

My uncle leant his chin on his hands and thought for a while. Just then I sensed a faint movement in the altar room – something black, like a shadow. I looked across and was horrified to see a dozen fat black rats hanging from the fretwork. I squinted at them and gradually realized they were not rats, but bats. They were staring at me with eerie, glinting eyes. Then, in the same room, I saw a human figure gently rise to its feet – a small, round-shouldered old woman with hair as white as morning snow. As she stood, the bats flew from the fretwork and gathered around her, some hanging from her shoulders and her waist. She stepped into the middle reception room, and suddenly turned towards us. Her face was round and child-like. A typically placid old lady, it would have seemed. But there was a fiery brightness in her eyes. They shone mysteriously, like those of a cat in the dark. And in the midst of her pale wrinkled face, her lips were red. I learned later that, even then, in her eighties, she applied rouge to her lips twice a day, using the finest safflower specially ordered from Yamagata. She looked at me. Her red lips slowly moved.

"House Number Three is empty, is it not?" she said.

She then moved into the middle reception room, closing the *fusuma* sliding screen behind her. One bat had been left inside the altar room. It flew at the closed screen, striking it forcefully with its long black wings. Then it flitted out to the veranda and from there disappeared into the middle reception room.

"That's true," my uncle muttered. "Number Three is empty. Do you want to stay there? Of course you'll have to do the same work as the labourers."

I nodded immediately. "Yes!" I said.

That was my first encounter with my uncle and grandmother.'

Inubuse picked up some tongs and stirred the ashes in the hearth, pushing hot embers together. He placed some kindling on the embers and hung the kettle on the hook above the hearth. He was obviously going to make some tea. Blue-white smoke billowed upwards as the kindling started to smoulder. He bent over the hearth, pushed his lips forward and blew on the embers.

'It looks like we're coming to the main part of the story,' I said, moving back from the heat of the fire. 'It's been rather a long introduction.'

Inubuse piled some wood on top of the kindling.

'Perhaps you're right,' he said. 'Getting the right balance requires discipline.'

'So that is how I ended up staying in House Number Three at Kuro Wood. Number Three was to the north of the main house and surrounded by aubergine fields. Everyone in the labourers' houses ate aubergines every day. We picked them, separated out the well-formed ones, and sent those to the main house. The rest we washed in Kiji River and ate raw with salt. We got our rations of rice from the kitchen – not white rice, of course; a dark mixture of three parts brown rice, four parts potato, and three parts kelp root.

After breakfast each day the labourers from each of the five huts went to the garden of the main house to hear my uncle's orders for the day.

"Weed the rice fields," he would say, or "Cut the grass on the hills."

We were then given lunch to take with us – two balls of kelp-rice and three shrivelled slices of pickled vegetable. Working with the labourers, I found out a lot about the main house. Gensaku from Number Two was a particularly good source of information.

"Have you seen the bats in the altar room?" I asked him one day in early autumn. We were very near here at the time, cutting grass for winter horse feed.'

While he spoke Inubuse's eyes were gazing out at the mountainside opposite the cave.

'"Yes, I've seen the bats," Gensaku said. "Everyone knows about the old lady's powers. Some people pay for them."

"Powers?"

"Discovering the unknown. That's what the bats are for. I've seen her do it," he said. "Say somebody's gone missing and people have done all they can to find them. They go to the old lady and ask for help. She goes out into the garden at night and brings the bats with her."

"And then?"

"She watches them fly, and she chants. From the way they fly she can tell where the missing person is."

"That's not possible!" I said.

"But she gets it right," said Gensaku. "There was a landowner who had lost an important bag – the old lady said where it would be and that's where it was found. I saw it with my own eyes."

At the time I didn't believe him. How could such an absurd story be true? If missing people and property could be found as simply as that, the police force would be out of a job.

While Gensaku and I were talking, a young woman walked up the hill towards us. She wore a simple blue-and-white kimono, in a style usually used by men. It was a ragged old garment, faded and patched. Yet it was spotlessly clean, and far from looking shabby it actually seemed rather fine. Her hair was long and parted in the middle. On her feet were rough straw sandals, which she had probably made herself.

Gensaku looked aghast.

"Shiho! What are you doing?" he said. "You must stay at home in bed!"

Her face was pale and translucent, and her lips were a strange red – like those of a patient at your sanatorium. But, although she looked sad, she was very beautiful, with fair skin and fine features.

"I've come for some lily roots," she said.

"Don't be foolish!" said Gensaku, waving her back. "What will happen if you're seen by someone from the main house? These mountains belong to them. They own every blade of grass, every root. If you take anything without permission you'll be beaten as a thief. You know that!"

"I thought you might like some boiled lily root, Father."

"Don't worry about me! Think about yourself!"

Shiho's shoulders sagged despondently at her father's harsh tone. She turned and went back down the path.

I had been there a month, but I had not noticed a young woman living next door. It was a strange oversight for a young man, but I suppose she had been sick in bed. Still, now that I'd seen her, I was extremely glad that I'd come to Kuro Wood.'

'You mean, you were in love with her,' I said.

'Perhaps,' said Inubuse, smiling sadly.

'Did you get anywhere?'

'Typical!' he said. 'You young people are always in a rush…'

He took the kettle from the hook and poured some water into the teapot.

'I had feelings for her, but she was an invalid. It was no time for courting.'

He poured some tea and placed a cup in front of me.

'Especially considering what happened that autumn…'

'Why? What happened?' I asked.

'There was an appalling famine,' he said. 'The region was hit by a series of powerful storms – typhoons we call them now – and the harvest was still worse than the year before, down by another third. The landowners tried to raise the rents, but the tenants protested. Once the landowners realised they couldn't squeeze another grain of rice from the farmers, most of them moved to Kamaishi, where the ironworks contributed enough to the town's finances to keep personal taxes low. As for the tenant farmers, all they could do to stay alive was sell their daughters. The number of girls in the district was shrinking all the time. Everybody noticed.

As labourers we were employed by the family, so the rent rises didn't affect us. But our tiny wages were cut repeatedly, until we were paid nothing at all. The amount of real rice in our rations fell too, so that in the end we ate almost nothing but roots. They told us if we didn't like it we could leave.

Eventually the snow came, and the estate was cut off. There was very little work to be done outside in the winter. Once a week we cleared snow off the roof of the main house. Sometimes we were sent to dig up vegetables that had been stored for the winter in holes in the fields. Sometimes we had to chase the horses out into the snowfields. But most of our time was spent making sacks in a shed by the storehouse beyond the garden. The sacks were sold to the fish market for waste, with all proceeds of course going to the family in the main house.

One morning in the middle of December, Gensaku didn't arrive on time for work in the shed. I felt uneasy. He was a hard worker and he had never once been late before, so why wasn't he here that day?

"Something's happened," I thought. "If my uncle knows he's late there'll be trouble."

So I went to Number Two to find him.

Opening the door, I noticed the bittersweet smell of a long-term sick room. Gensaku was kneeling beside Shiho, looking intently at her face.

"What's the matter?" I asked.

He moved his swollen eyes slowly towards me.

"She's very ill," he said.

Shiho's face was red – a strange, unhealthy flush. Her eyelids were slightly open, her gaze fixed on the ceiling, her eyes not moving at all. Her breathing was weak and rapid.

"She hasn't spoken for ten days. She hasn't the energy."

Gensaku was holding her hand under the futon. Her breathing quickened. He put his mouth to her ear.

"You'll be all right," he said loudly. "Your dad's here with you. You're going to get well. Is there anything you'd like me to do? If I can do it, I will. Just tell me."

She didn't reply; she just lay panting like a tired dog.

Gensaku gave up and lifted his head. He smiled weakly.

"She's been like this the whole time."

"Has a doctor seen her?" I asked.

Gensaku shook his head feebly.

"You must get one," I said. "I'll talk to my uncle. I'll borrow some money from him."

But as I stood up to leave, Shiho spoke. Her voice was unexpectedly firm.

"No!" she said. "You mustn't borrow money because of me. It will only mean Father suffering…"

Then, with a dream-like look, she murmured: "I don't have long. But before I die I would like just once to have a taste of white rice gruel…"

Gensaku rubbed his eyes with the backs of his hands.

"Is that all?" he cried. "You open your mouth for the first time in ten days and ask only for that? Such a simple thing! Gruel!"

But I knew that there nothing simple about it. How was white rice to be obtained in the middle of a famine? Nobody knew the difficulty better than Gensaku. He certainly didn't have the money to buy any, and while there was probably a sack or two hidden in one of the estate's five storehouses, my uncle wasn't the type to let anyone have so much as a handful at a time like this. If someone had asked him, he would have shouted at them for suggesting such an extravagance. In fact, he might have thrown them out there and then, glad of the opportunity to cut the number of mouths to feed.'

Inubuse sighed deeply. He sat in silence for a long while, his eyes resting on the fire in the hearth. He looked reluctant to say any more.

'And then? What happened next?' I said, unable to stay silent any longer.

'That evening one of the storehouses was broken into, and two pounds of white rice were stolen from a sack.'

'It was Gensaku, wasn't it,' I said.

'Well, yes. I knew who'd done it as soon as I heard the rice was missing.'

'And did they find out?' I asked.

'I kept quiet and pretended not to know anything about it. Nobody found out until the following evening.'

'What happened then?'

'All the labourers and kitchen maids were summoned in the snow to the garden. My uncle must have decided that the culprit was an employee – a real thief wouldn't take just two pounds of rice, he would take at least a whole sack.

We waited for my uncle to appear, trying to keep warm by stamping on the ground in our straw boots. After about an hour the door clattered open. To our surprise, instead of my uncle, it was my grandmother who came out to the veranda. As soon as she appeared, black shapes emerged in the air around her. The bats. They flitted and screeched above our heads. Then suddenly, with astonishing speed, they flew down towards us, each aiming for a different person. They stopped about a metre in front of their targets' eyes, turned lightly around and disappeared like *ninja* into the darkness. Then, before we knew it, other bats were flying towards us. We dived down onto the snow, our arms over our heads to keep the bats at bay. During a brief lull in the onslaught, I managed to lift my head high enough to see my grandmother standing on the veranda. She was holding prayer beads and seemed to be chanting to herself. The sinister brightness in her eyes grew stronger. She was staring fixedly at someone near me. I followed her gaze and realised that her eyes were on Gensaku. He was kneeling on the ground, his arms dangling loosely in front of him like a marionette. He was trembling. By the light of the veranda, his face seemed whiter than the snow.

"Come!" cried my grandmother, beckoning to the bats. In a moment they were all back inside the house. She watched them go in, then slid the door firmly shut.'

'What happened next...?' I asked. Unconsciously edging closer to Inubuse, I knocked a tea cup with my knee and it rattled across the floor.

'The next morning Gensaku was dead, the top half of his body submerged in Kiji River.'

Inubuse spoke quickly as though the matter was distasteful to him.

'A lot of people freeze to death in these parts. They get drunk and fall asleep in the snow. People said that's what happened to Gensaku, but I can't believe it.'

'Why not?' I said.

'For one thing, he didn't have the money to buy drink. And there was a wound in his throat – I saw it with my own eyes. It looked as though something sharp had ripped into his flesh. Because he was in the river, there was no bloodstain on the snow. In other words...'

'...He'd been pushed down into the river so that no bloodstains would be left.'

The old man nodded.

'It was a bat, wasn't it, that got his throat.'

The old man shook his head.

'I don't know. Maybe it was, but then again, maybe it wasn't. But why would Gensaku have gone a hundred metres from his own house to Kiji River? I've wondered about that for the past thirty years. But I still don't understand...'

His voice trailed off.

'Don't you think he must have been chased by the bats?'

Inubuse didn't respond. He picked up the tongs and wrote something in the ashes of the hearth, then erased it straight away. He wrote it again, and again erased it.

'What happened to Shiho?' I asked.

'She recovered,' he said. 'Strangely, she recovered completely. In the new year, she started work as a maid in the kitchen of the main house. In her spare time she would go to the part of the river where Gensaku died. She would stand on the bank and cry and cry.

After a while, she stopped speaking. I don't know whether she didn't want to speak, or whether so much crying had damaged her throat, but for a long time she said nothing to anybody. Then spring came and she was joined by a companion. He wondered in one day and ended up staying.'

'…He?'

'Perhaps I should say "it". Her companion was a pheasant.'

'…A pheasant?'

'It had a wounded leg. Shiho looked after the pheasant and its leg got better. From then on it was always with her. When she went to the kitchen, it followed her. If she went to the mountain, it led the way. But one day the pheasant and the bats started fighting. There was no particular reason; it just suddenly happened – and the pheasant ended up killing every one of the bats. My grandmother collapsed in a fit when she heard. My uncle was furious too and went out with his gun to shoot it. But it was hiding and he couldn't find it, so he gave up and went back inside. When Shiho came out of the kitchen, though, the pheasant was so pleased to see her that it came out from its hiding place and began to crow. My uncle heard it, and came outside once more. He aimed his gun at the noise and fired. The pheasant fell down into the garden.

Shiho ran over to the pheasant, picked it up in her arms and held it to her cheek. Then for the first time in months she spoke: "All I did was tell Father I wanted some gruel. All you did was tell me where you were. We just opened our mouths…"

I ran towards her.

"Shiho, you can speak!"

She looked at me steadily, and then turning away, ran towards the mountain. I sensed something deeply wrong and ran after her.'

'And then?'

Inubuse pointed towards the azaleas on the mountainside opposite the cave.

'I lost sight of her over there. I never saw her again. The azaleas were in flower then too...'

As I listened I wondered if Inubuse had come to live here so that he could look for Shiho, the girl who had disappeared thirty years before. I wondered if his trumpeting was in fact a call to her.

But time was up – I had to get back to the sanatorium, so I decided not to ask. I bowed to Inubuse and went outside.

I looked at the azaleas on the mountainside. They were brighter than they had been an hour before. Or so it seemed to me.

馬

Horse

It was a hot Saturday at the start of my first summer at the sanatorium. As soon as I heard Inubuse's trumpet I left work and walked along the mountain path to his cave. It took only five minutes, but by the time I arrived I was drenched in sweat. I dived into the cool cave and started mopping my face with a handkerchief.

'What a lot of sweat!' Inubuse said. 'You look like a horse after a gallop. Sweat pours off horses in hot weather.'

'I'm glad I'm *not* a horse,' I said. 'Horses can't wipe their sweat away!'

I gulped back the cup of water the old man had given me. It was spring water fresh from the rocks, and tasted faintly of grass.

'They can cool themselves though,' he said. 'In rivers and lakes, or in the sea. Let me tell you a story about it.'

I nodded and was settling down to listen when Inubuse suddenly stood up.

'If I'm to talk about horses cooling themselves,' he said, 'we should go to Maki Point.'

I had heard of Maki Point. It was a promontory of thirty-metre high cliffs a few kilometres south of Kamaishi.

'That's fine for me,' I said, 'but won't it be difficult for you to get home? It's three or four kilometres from the cape to Kamaishi and another six from Kamaishi to here. That's ten kilometres each way. It'll be night-time before you get back.'

'You've no sense of direction, have you,' he laughed. 'Maki's certainly a long way if you go via Kamaishi. But it's pretty close as the crow flies.'

He used his tongs to sketch a triangle in the cold ashes of the hearth, then pointed the tongs at the narrowest angle.

'Kamaishi is here at the thirty-degree angle.'

He moved the tongs to the widest angle.

'Maki Cape is here at the right-angle.'

He then ran the tongs back along the line towards the first angle and from there to the third angle.

'This sixty-degree angle is where we are now.'

'Obviously,' he continued, 'if you go down from here to the thirty-degree angle and then up to the right-angle, it's a long way. But if you go direct from the sixty-degree angle to the right-angle, it's very close.'

'I suppose so,' I said. 'But it must be tough walking.'

'Not at all,' he said. 'There's only one mountain to cross. There was a busy roadway over to Maki before the war. People and horses were coming and going all the time.'

I followed Inubuse out of the cave and we set off east through the bright summer sunlight. The leaves were green and fresh, and we could smell the grass as we walked. A few days earlier everything had been wet with rain, but the season seemed to have changed. I could see a bank of white summer cloud above the green outline of the hill in front of us. Amongst the lush summer grass at our feet were specks of bright red.

'Wild strawberries!' said Inubuse, bending to pick one. 'Horses love these. People can eat them too, of course.'

He tossed the berry into his mouth. I copied him. The taste was sharp and acidic.

We stopped for a while at the top of the hill. Inubuse pointed straight ahead.

'Before the war Maki Point was used as pastureland for horses,' he said.

Beneath the blue sky and white cloud were the green waves of the Pacific Ocean. And projecting out into the sea was a small cape, about one kilometre in length. It was shaped like a *shamoji* – a spatula for serving rice.

'It's perfect for keeping horses, isn't it,' said Inubuse.

I know nothing of horses, but I immediately understood what he meant. The horses could run free on the wide end of the cape, bounded on three sides by the sea. And the narrow handle-like part, less than fifty metres across, would be easy to fence.

'In 1935,' Inubuse told me, 'there would have been forty to fifty half-wild mares down there.'

He started walking down a pathway directly towards the cape. To our left we could make out, through some cedar trees, the southern tip of Kamaishi. To our right was a village of some sixty houses, stretched out along the edge of the sea.

'With those fifty mares,' he continued, 'there would have been just three or four stallions.'

'Who owned the pasture?'

He gestured with his chin to the village on our right.

'*They* did.'

'You mean the village?'

'That's right. Every year the villagers would gather the young horses and take them up this way to the horse market at Tono. It brought them a lot of money. And when I lived there the army came to buy horses direct from the village.'

'You lived in the village?'

Inubuse gazed down towards the houses, nodding sadly.

'I taught at the village school for about a year,' he said.

Then with a speed and sure-footedness that seemed remarkable for a man of his age, he continued straight down the hill to the cape.

The wide end of the cape was covered with young cedar trees. On either side, sheer cliffs fell tens of metres to the sea. I followed Inubuse down a pathway to the shore – the only place on the cape where you reach the sea by foot.

'This is where the horses cooled themselves off,' said Inubuse, sitting down on a rock at the bottom of the slope.

I took off my shoes, dipped my feet in the cold water and looked back up towards the old pasture. It had been odd to see so much grass between the young cedars – grass does not normally grow easily amongst trees.

'When it was used for pasture there were no trees there at all,' said Inubuse, reading my thoughts. 'It was just grass the whole way across. The wood started at the neck of the cape and that's where the horses slept at night. In winter they lived there all the time, to shelter from the cold. They ate leaves, buds and plants in the wood.'

'Why was the grassland planted with cedars?'

'The villagers must have thought there would be more money in forestry than horses. There are no horses left now. After the war no one wanted horses, especially not the type that was kept here – small and half-wild. They'd been very good for farm work and pulling carts, and the army found them excellent for transporting munitions. They were nimble, strong and hard-working, and they'd eat anything. But after the war their work was taken by trucks and tractors.'

Inubuse looked towards the village, shielding his eyes from the sun. The houses squatted in a row in the narrow space between the mountains and the sea.

'Can you see the temple in the middle?' he asked.

I nodded. The red tiles of the temple stood out against the plain zinc roofs of the other houses.

'That's Shinkoji Temple. I rented a room there when I was teaching at the school. The priest of the temple was also the village headman. Next door to the temple lived a cart-man called Gentaro and his daughter Aoe. Gentaro's horse was a fine, small, stocky stallion called Shiro.'

'Sounds like a dog,' I said. Shiro, or 'White', was a common name for dogs.

'Yes,' said Inubuse. 'Well, he was as faithful as a dog. He also had a large white mark on his forehead and four white socks. Aoe used to call him Shirou, making his name sound like a man's. My story today is about Shiro and Aoe's love suicide.'

I looked at him in astonishment. A love suicide between a horse and a human! He had to be joking. But his face was so sad he might have been staring into the depths of hell.

'It was a love suicide right enough,' he said. 'You'll understand if you listen to what I say.'

'But the idea of a human and a horse committing love suicide is too ridiculous,' I said.

'You appear to be steeped in a thoroughly corrupt modernism,' said Inubuse, solemnly stroking his unshaven chin. 'You people have no true contact with Nature. You avoid it. You only deal with the artificial and as a result you've lost all understanding of Nature, and of the animals that live within it. Before this rampant artificiality – what you seem to call 'culture' or 'civilization', intimacy between horses and humans was seen as perfectly normal. Take this incident in Tono, for example. It's well documented. About a hundred years ago a rich man died, leaving a wife and daughter. Both were extremely beautiful and all the men of the town competed for their favours. They all wooed them and some tried to get into their rooms at night. But the women resisted every one of them. In fact, they paid them not the slightest attention. The reason they had no appetite for men was that they had another kind of lover – their horse.'

'Their horse?'

'Yes. There was a witness. One man who was obsessed with the daughter spent the night watching their stable. The daughter came to the stable at nightfall and slipped off her kimono in front of the horse's nose. The horse snorted, flaring its nostrils and pounding the ground with his hooves. "Good boy," said the girl gently, stroking his penis and caressing it with her mouth. Then they made passionate love. A short while later the girl left the stable, the mother quietly entered and said to the horse, "Do to me what you did to my daughter…"'

'Well I never…' I said, shifting my position.

'The man who was watching was Sanaemon Yamada, the heir to a rich farmer in Tono. He wrote a diary called the *Journal of Sanaemon*. He relates this story in his entry for February 3, 1864. A short while later, apparently, the horse wasted away and died.

'Now,' continued Inubuse, returning to his own narrative, 'I won't explain why I was working at the village school; it has nothing to do with the story and will just slow things down.

I moved to the village from Kamaishi towards the end of winter, arriving at the Shinkoji Temple with a single wicker trunk. I'd got a lift with Gentaro, who was bringing goods to the village general store on his horse-drawn sleigh.

It was harsh weather for late March, and at every step Shiro's straw-clad legs sank knee-deep into the snow. Gentaro sat on the sleigh with the reins in one hand and a large bottle of *shochu* liquor in the other.

"On! On! Shiro!" he shouted. "Aoe's waiting for you!"

And Shiro, like a steam train, emitted a powerful blast of white air from his nostrils and chugged on with extraordinary energy across the expanse of snow. Every time Gentaro shouted "Aoe," Shiro thrust all his strength down into his pounding legs, as though he were engaged in some fierce battle with the snowfields. It was a fine sight.

"Who is Aoe?" I asked.

Gentaro leered.

"My daughter," he said. "Shiro's in love with her. Hearing her name stirs him up."

At the time I thought the man was being stupid, but when we reached the village something happened to support what he had said. As soon as the sleigh stopped outside the temple, I heard an excited voice shout "Shirou! Shirou!" and a beautiful, large-framed girl came running out of Gentaro's house next door. This of course was Aoe. She hugged Shiro's neck and rubbed her cheek against his mane, kissing him, and stroking his back. Shiro in turn licked her hair, face, and neck. Standing side to side in opposite directions, they nuzzled each other, just like two horses.

"That's enough!" shouted Gentaro. "There's nothing to be done with this bastard Shiro, but you, Aoe, you should behave yourself proper in front of people. Nobody'll marry you if you carry on like that!"

"I'm not going to marry," said Aoe, still stroking Shiro's neck. "It wouldn't be fair to Shirou."

Shiro turned his face towards Gentaro, whinnying and baring his teeth. It was almost as if he was laughing.

"You pile of shit!" shouted Gentaro, whipping the reins against Shiro's flank in a drunken fury. "A filthy animal drooling over my daughter! Makes me sick!"

Shiro showed not the slightest fear, and, turning his head once more, stared at Gentaro with cold malice.

"Stop it, Dad!" said Aoe, grabbing the reins and jumping up into the sleigh. "I'll take the goods to the store. Go inside and have another drink!"

Aoe shook the reins and Shiro trotted lightly off, his neck stretched forward, his legs lifting high at each step. The horse bells gradually faded into the winter evening.

The bad weather did not let up for three days. On the evening of the third day I opened the study window and was gazing disconsolately out at the endless snow when I heard bells in the distance. It was a damp, muted sound, the tinkle of the horse bells muffled by the falling snow. The door of Gentaro's house opened and out ran Aoe in straw snow-boots.

"Shirou! Shirou!" she cried.

I imagined that she would again nuzzle with Shiro, and that Gentaro would again scold her for damaging her marriage prospects. I was about to close the window when Aoe shouted:

"Shirou! Where's Dad?"

Other people had heard her shout and were gathering outside. I joined them, thinking that something must be wrong.

"Shirou!" sobbed Aoe, shaking Shiro's head from side to side. "What on earth has happened to Dad? Tell me!"

Shiro licked the nape of Aoe's neck. The cold light that had shone in his eyes three evenings before was gone; his expression was now calm and gentle.

All that was on the sleigh was the rabbit-fur flying cap that Gentaro always wore. The priest led the village fire brigade in a search party and they found Gentaro's frozen body that night, floating in the water at the tip of the cape.

"How did he die?" I asked later that night when the priest returned from the cape.

"He fell from the sleigh when he was drunk," said the priest.

"How do you know?"

"He was always drinking, so people had thought this might happen. He was still clutching a *shochu* bottle when we found him – what better evidence could there be? The villagers are saying that it was the perfect end for someone who loved his drink so much."

"But might there be another explanation?" I said. "What if Shiro deliberately made a sharp turn so that Gentaro would fall from the sleigh? Gentaro was drunk, so Shiro would have expected him to fall asleep in the snow and die of exposure. And what actually happened was that he fell from the cape, ensuring no chance of survival."

The priest knitted his thick eyebrows, and rubbed his bald head.

"Have you checked the sleigh marks in the snow?" I asked.

"No," he said. "It's too dark to do that. And in this weather any marks would be quickly covered by fresh snow anyway."

"Shiro planned the perfect crime," I said.

"But Mr Inubuse, why would Shiro do such a thing?"

"He's in love with Aoe," I said. "The day before yesterday Gentaro got very angry about it and whipped him, so Shiro had a grudge. And, of course, with Gentaro out of the way Shiro can woo Aoe as much as he wants. So really he's got two birds with one stone."

The priest burst out laughing.

"Mr Inubuse, you tell jokes with such a straight face!"

"It's no joke," I said. "I saw the murderous hatred in Shiro's eyes."

He laughed still louder.

"Mr Inubuse, you're talking about a horse! However clever a horse may be, it's hardly going to think up a plot like that!"

And so Gentaro's death was treated as a simple case of exposure, for which he himself was to blame.'

While Inubuse was telling his story, I'd been sitting on a rock, with my feet in the water. I suddenly noticed that the tide was coming in and the water had risen from my ankles to my shins. I hurriedly moved to another rock, nearer the cliff.

'Aoe took over her father's carting business. There was plenty of work to do; Shiro was very obedient and Aoe looked after him very well. This was probably the happiest time they had together.'

Here Inubuse tapped his pipe against a rock, signalling a change of mood.

'When May came around, it was decided that a stallion should be put to stud among the mares in the pasture. There was a meeting about it at the temple. The villagers eventually drew lots and it fell to Aoe to provide the stallion. According to ancient rules, she could not refuse. In tears, she released Shiro into the pasture.'

'I'm surprised Shiro went along with it,' I said. 'Aoe was human so she may have listened to people's arguments, but I can't help thinking it would be difficult to persuade a horse.'

'Well,' said Inubuse, 'there were problems. I'm not sure how he did it, but Shiro got over the fence and came straight back home to Aoe. He was caught and taken back to the pasture. But again the next morning he was back eating the grass outside Aoe's house. So it was decided that Shiro could, as it were, commute to the pasture. Aoe would take Shiro to the pasture in the mornings, and bring him home again in the evenings, when his work was over.'

'Aoe wouldn't have been able to do her cart work without Shiro,' I said.

'That's right.'

'So how did she get money?'

'She received a fair amount when Shiro was bought by the village. And because she was spending her days at the pasture, the village paid her a small daily allowance. So she had no immediate problem supporting herself. But there was still a problem in the pasture. When Aoe was with him Shiro would not mate with the mares. And if she wasn't there, he would just come home. So either way he didn't do his job as a sire. And of course there is a season for mating – if the season is missed there are no foals in the autumn – so the priest and villagers began to get worried. One evening the priest came to my room.

"Mr Inubuse," he said, coming straight to the point, "it must be inconvenient for you being single. Are you considering taking a wife?"

"Not at the moment," I said.

His shoulders sagged in disappointment.

"I was actually wondering whether Aoe might be suitable for you."

"Aoe?'

"She's a good-looking girl…"

She was beautiful, in fact. Her features were stronger than most Japanese women's. I'm sure she had *shirako* blood. You must have seen those striking girls on the coast with fair skin and large dark eyes. They're descendants of the *shirako* children born between Russian sailors and Japanese women.

"She is very healthy," said the priest, "and she works extremely hard. I'm sure she would prove a good wife. What do you think?"

I took the idea seriously. There was something rough about her, but she seemed a pleasant enough girl. She might well make a good wife. I was almost forty and if I didn't marry soon I might miss my chance.

"Let me think about it," I said.

The priest rubbed his bald head cheerfully.

Later that week, on Saturday afternoon – it was a very hot day for May – I took a walk down to the cape. When I got there I sat down. Some of the horses were on their backs rubbing their coats to get rid of fleas. It was a comical sight. While I was watching their performance I heard Aoe's voice coming from the shore where we are now. She was laughing happily – a particular type of laugh, the laugh of a woman who is enjoying the physical companionship of her favourite man.

I came down from the pasture towards the shore. Aoe was in the sea, completely naked. Shiro was beside her, gently and carefully licking her naked white skin. He seemed to be getting excited. He threw his head up in the air, bared his teeth and flared his nostrils. At the same time he urinated. Later I found out that this is exactly how horses behave before they mate.

I have a vivid memory of this scene – a horse and human cavorting together in the early summer sea. Strangely, there seemed nothing lewd in it. On the contrary, it seemed entirely natural and proper.

I left quietly so as not to disturb them.

That night I spoke to the priest.

"It's about Aoe… I think I must say no."

"But why? You seem very suited to one another. There's a difference in age, of course, but… Are you saying you don't like her?"

"No, in fact I would be happy be to marry her, but I know she would never agree to marry me – she loves another man."

"Another man…?'

"Another male, to be more accurate."

"…"

"Shiro and Aoe are in love with each other."

The priest looked angry.

"How very imaginative, Mr Inubuse," he said tersely, and, turning on his heels, he walked straight out of the room.

A few days later, three soldiers came to the village from Morioka to buy transport horses for the army. Coming back from work in the afternoon I found the temple grounds in a great clamour. A dozen horses that the soldiers had bought were tied to stakes. They were neighing and pounding the ground with their hooves. To my surprise, one of the horses was Shiro. I guessed the priest had given up on Shiro as a sire and had decided to replace him in the pasture with another stallion.

I heard Aoe's voice. She was on the verge of tears, pleading with the soldiers as they sat cross-legged in front of the main temple building.

"Shiro was originally my horse! Please let me buy him back!"

"Where is your patriotism?" shouted a soldier with a corporal's badge, rising heavily to his feet. "These horses have been bought by the Imperial Army, so watch what you say! They belong to His Imperial Highness! How dare you ask to buy one back?"

"But…" persisted Aoe, "I still I want to buy him, whatever!"

"Traitor!" cried the corporal.

Grabbing her chin with his left hand he pulled her face up towards him. His right hand rose swiftly up as though to strike her. He was a soldier – there was nothing I could do to stop him. I closed my eyes, imagining the pain she would feel, bracing myself for the sound of his palm hitting her cheek. But the sound did not come. What had happened? I opened my eyes nervously. The corporal was leering at Aoe's face.

"Quite a beauty…" he mewed. "In view of your *qualities*… I may be able to reconsider."

"You mean you'll let me buy Shiro back?"

"Perhaps I will…"

"…Thank you."

"But there is a condition. I'm staying in the guest quarters of the temple.. Bring me some *sake* this evening. If you serve it well, I may consider your request. What do you say?"

Aoe looked towards Shiro, tied to the stake. He kicked the ground vigorously. She turned back to the corporal and solemnly nodded her head.'

Suddenly a cool breeze got up. The sun had disappeared behind the mountains to the west. The tide was rising quickly and Inubuse and I had to move still closer to the cliff.

'What happened next?' I asked.

'The matter ran its course,' Inubuse replied. 'Naturally, the corporal had no intention of granting Aoe's request. He was just playing her along. The plan was simply that she'd serve him some *sake* in his room, and when the opportunity arose he'd jump her.'

'So, she went to the corporal's room and…'

'Don't work yourself up,' said the old man, lifting his hands to calm me. He smoked his pipe for a while.

'Well,' he said eventually, tapping the pipe again on the edge of a rock, 'that night I was reading a book in my room – it must have been about eight o' clock – when I heard a cry from the guest quarters.

"Help me, Shiro!" Aoe was shouting. "Shiro! Come quickly!"

I stood up, listening intently, trying to ascertain what was happening. Just then something white, like a butterfly, passed in front of my window. In the darkness I couldn't tell what it was, but it was certainly something white.

What I had seen was the mark on Shiro's forehead. I don't know how he had got away from his stake, but he was free and had just gone past my window. A few moments later from the guest quarters I heard the sound of doors and screens being smashed down, and a terrified cry from the corporal.

Then all was quiet. In trepidation I put my head out of the window and looked through the darkness towards the guest quarters. The calm clip-clop of Shiro's hooves approached and passed by. Shiro was carrying Aoe by a kimono sash held in his mouth. The priest ran into the guest quarters to find the corporal with a bloody gash across his forehead. He was dead.

Early the next morning, on the orders of the two remaining soldiers, we began to search for Shiro and Aoe. They were soon found. Up there.'

Inubuse pointed to the top of the high cliff to his left.

'The soldiers led the way with their pistols. We followed with sticks, hoes, and shovels. Shiro looked afraid as we approached. He kept circling Aoe, who was lying on the grass.

The fresh spring grass looked dark, and the scent of the morning dew mingled with the smell of blood. Aoe was naked from the waist down, and her pale skin was stained crimson. She was motionless. The soldiers aimed their pistols at Shiro's white forehead. For a moment he stopped moving. Then he took Aoe's kimono sash in his mouth and lifted her off the ground, holding her just as he had on the previous evening. He trotted seven or eight paces to the edge of the cliff and from there, like Pegasus, he leapt towards the sky.'

Inubuse looked again at the cliff to his left. It was thirty metres high. Rough waves were breaking at its base.

After a while I spoke:

'The lower half of Aoe's body was bloody because… I mean, did Shiro do to her what a man does to a woman?'

'Nobody knows the details,' said Inubuse, standing up. 'But I am sure that did indeed happen.'

The shades of the sea, sky, and grass darkened as evening came. We climbed the steep slope from the shore and stood on the edge of the cliff where Shiro and Aoe had ended their lives. The cliff top was covered in horse clover. I pulled up a handful and threw it to the wind over the sea.

狐
Fox

'What kind of story would you like today?'

Inubuse was sitting cross-legged beside the fireless hearth. He tapped his pipe on the hearth edge as he spoke.

'Anything at all,' I said, sitting down opposite him.

It was midday at the height of summer. Outside the sun was blazing and the air as hot as the cauldron of hell, but the interior of the cave was pleasantly cool. My sweat chilled on my skin, soothing away the uncomfortable heat.

From a distance came a sound like the crack of snapping bamboo.

'Daytime fireworks,' said Inubuse.

He opened the fly-proof cupboard fixed to the wall of the cave, took out a plate of *edamame* beans and placed it on the edge of the hearth. His lunch.

'I wonder where the fireworks are,' he said. 'Sadanai River?'

Sadanai River is between the sanatorium and Kamaishi. It is a small, fast-flowing river that runs into the Pacific.

'Yes,' I said. 'There's a display there tonight. I saw a flier on an electricity pole on my way to the sanatorium. I suppose they're setting some off now to whet people's appetites for this evening.'

'A firework display…'

Inubuse's hand paused in mid-air, a pod of beans suspended from his fingers. His eyes seemed to be set on something far away.

'A firework display…' he muttered again. His tone was flat and listless.

'Is there something about a firework display which…?' I tailed off, hoping to prompt a reaction.

'Well…' said the old man, his gaze settling on my face. 'The word "fireworks" reminded me of someone – a woman called Oyone.'

He rapidly popped the beans out of the pod and into his mouth. He must have been well over sixty, but his teeth looked as strong as a horse's. A light green piece of bean was stuck between two of his teeth. He rinsed some barley tea around his mouth and the bean was gone. He poured some barley tea for me.

'Who was Oyone?' I asked, as I sipped the tea.

He smiled faintly.

'She was my wife.'

'Ah!' I said. 'What kind of woman was she?'

'She was kind, hard-working and beautiful. The perfect woman.'

He sighed deeply.

'There was just one thing wrong with her,' he said quietly.

'What was that?'

'She was possessed by a fox.'

I stared at him.

'Possessed by a fox?'

He nodded.

'There were a lot of foxes around here when we were young, so in the villages nearby there were always one or two people who were possessed. Oyone was one of them.'

We heard another firework in the distance.

'In fact, she was more than possessed.'

'What do you mean?'

Inubuse did not reply. He seemed lost in thought.

'There was a firework display the night I first met Oyone,' he muttered.

'Don't beat about the bush,' I said. 'Tell me about her!'

'All right,' he said, flicking another bean into his mouth.

He took a slurp of barley tea and rinsed it noisily around his teeth.

'I told you I worked as a teacher in a school in a village to the south of Kamaishi. Well, I gave up that job and joined a tailor's – the largest in Kamaishi. I was a salesman – a type of peddler, really.'

He hunched up as though carrying something heavy on his back.

'I lived at the shop and had two main tasks. One was delivering clothes to customers; the other was sales trips to surrounding villages. I went on several trips each month, carrying material on my back in a wicker trunk. I liked going. It meant I didn't have to worry about what the boss was thinking, or get involved in colleagues' gossip. I conversed with the sky, the clouds and the road. During the day I worked very hard at selling and at night I stayed at simple guesthouses in the mountain villages. I didn't have to fit in with anybody. I was on a little journey of my own, free to do as I pleased. I even took on trips that my colleagues didn't want to make. I worked as hard as I could, and things went well. If you enjoy something, you tend to succeed, and after a year I had built up a good set of customers – three or four landowners from this village, four or five old families from that village and so on. I took material that would appeal to them personally.

"I have brought you a lovely piece of Oshima, sir. I think it will suit you very well."

"I put this striped crepe in my trunk, madam – I thought it was just the thing for you."

"I've a school kimono for your son. It's the finest quality cloth – made in Okayama. What do you think?"

"I've hunted down a pattern that would be perfect for your daughter."

"How about this silk for your maids? It's a little faded, but I can take account of that in the price."

If you target well, you sell well. I got a good reputation in the villages – "Inubuse," they said, "he cares about us." I'd go back to the shop with an empty trunk and the boss would raise my commission. Everything was going well and soon I was the top salesman in the company. It was then that I met Oyone.'

Inubuse filled his pipe and lit it. The cave filled with the smell of mugwort, which he had mixed with his tobacco. He said that it tasted good and saved money.

'Perhaps you know a little bay called Toni to the south of Kamaishi?' he asked.

I nodded. It is a quiet inlet surrounded by pine trees where we used to swim as children.

'The river that runs into Toni Bay is the Kumano. Upriver is the village of Arakane. The afternoon I first arrived in Arakane fireworks were being let off, just like today. I didn't have any idea why there were fireworks, as I wasn't familiar with the area. Most of my trips up until then had been to the north and west of Kamaishi – to Ozuchi, for example, and the area around Tono.

"That sounds like fireworks," I said to the wife of a landowner in Arakane as I unrolled some cloth from my trunk. "Is there a celebration?"

"There's a new bridge over the river," the lady told me, taking the cloth up between her fingers for inspection. "The previous bridge was swept away in a flood the year before last. We've waited a year and ten months for this new bridge and getting across the river has been very difficult. But the problems are over now that the new bridge is complete."

Still holding the cloth, she gestured towards the garden. I turned around and between some green trees I saw the blue of the river in the distance. Over the river was a long wooden bridge.

"There's a firework display this evening to celebrate the new bridge. Why don't you come and watch from here? You'll have an excellent view."

Arakane was quite a small village with only about a hundred households, so I guessed it was the first time they had ever had a firework display. The lady, who was about fifty, was obviously very excited.

"Please do come!" she said.

I refused politely. This was salesman's instinct. People are kind to you and later try to take advantage of it, asking for special discounts. I sold her a few kimono collars, and then visited another five or six houses before the sun began to sink behind the mountains. It hadn't been a very successful day.

"I shouldn't have come south," I muttered as I put down my trunk at the guesthouse by the river. "I haven't sold a single roll of cloth."

I sat down in my sooty eight-mat room and began to devour my supper. Suddenly there was a tremendous whoosh, and a firework shot up from the riverbed outside. For a moment everything was as bright as day.

Feeling rather hot, I went outside for a stroll and started to walk across the new bridge. It was packed with people watching the fireworks. Arakane is in the middle of nowhere of course, so their firework display was a very basic one. There were just a couple of ten- or twenty-centimetre crowns. And even those were set off one at a time – no multiples, no overlaps, no speed firing. There were no multi-coloured stars or special shapes in the first half. It was just full stars, single-colour. "Full stars" means either a shower of stars or a star that explodes in different directions – they're very simple, dull devices. In the second half they managed three multi-colours and three shapes.

I reached the other side of the bridge and wandered along the embankment. I had one eye on the fireworks and the other on the girls in the crowd, but neither was much to look at, so I thought I'd go back to the guesthouse for some *sake*. As I set off back across the bridge I heard a voice.

"Ooh! How lovely!"

I looked and saw a young woman gazing up at the firework that had just been let off. It was the first multi-colour of the evening, an *ingenboshi*. It had small red stars followed by small green stars. The reason they appear at different times is because of a special type of gunpowder that burns without giving off light. This is pasted over the green stars so that, although both red and green stars are burning, at first you can only see the red stars. I know about fireworks because I once worked in a firework factory – I'll tell you about it another time.

I could see the girl's face quite clearly in the light of the firework. She was standing on her own about two metres away looking up at the sky, totally absorbed in what she saw. She had a fine oval face and large eyes. I was still gazing at her when the green stars disappeared and everything once again became pitch-black. The girl's fair-skinned face remained just visible, a vague white in the darkness.

Another firework shot up. This time it was reasonably sophisticated, with red and blue concentric circles, like a snake's eye. This was the highlight of the evening. The crowd in the riverbed roared. The girl gasped. I looked at the side of her face and made a decision there and then.

"That's the girl I'm going to marry!" I told myself. "I must find out her name and where she lives."

I waited for the light from the snake's eye to disappear. Then I took two paces in her direction and said, "Beautiful fireworks, aren't they, young lady?"

There was no reply. I could have kicked myself – only a tart would respond to a line like that.

"Don't worry," I said. "There's nothing odd about me. I work at Tanroku Tailors in Kamaishi."

I thought this would reassure her. Tanroku Tailors was a large and reputable store, well-known in the area.

But still there was no reply.

I looked again in her direction and to my astonishment I realised I was looking into complete darkness. She was no longer there. In the time it took me to utter those few words, she had mysteriously vanished.

Another firework went off – a simple one-colour device. It lit up the river bed as bright as day. I quickly looked all around, but no one was moving – either on the bridge or on the riverbed. Everybody was standing still, looking at the firework.'

'That's strange,' I said to Inubuse. 'If she had just left you would have seen her moving away – particularly if everybody else was still.'

'I couldn't see her at all,' Inubuse said, and then he grinned. 'But I wasn't too disappointed. I thought she must live in the village because she was wearing only a light *yukata* robe, and wooden clogs. As a clothing peddler I could get into any house, and so if I went round every house in the village I would be sure to meet her again.'

'And did you?'

'Yes I did,' he said.

He tapped his pipe vigorously against the edge of the hearth.

'She lived in a big house on the outskirts of the village. She was an only child. Her father had been a hunter when he was young and rumour had it that while out in the mountains he had come across a small gold deposit, which he had sold for a fortune to a mining company. Now he lived in a house like a castle. It backed onto the mountainside, and just on the border between his garden and the mountain was a shrine dedicated to Inari, the fox deity.

'So what did you do once you'd found out where she lived?' I asked.

'I started going to Arakane every week. My boss and colleagues were suspicious, of course. "Why does he go there every week? It's a tiny place. He must know they won't buy much." But I wasn't bothered by their gossip. I just kept going back, to meet the girl.'

Inubuse poured more barley tea into his cup from the kettle. The cup overflowed onto his lap, but he didn't notice – he seemed completely absorbed in his memories.

'One afternoon in early autumn, about a month after the firework display, I was on the veranda of their house in Arakane, showing some cloth to the girl's father, when he suddenly said:

"You're fond of Oyone, aren't you?"

My hands froze on the cloth. I was startled. His words exposed my deepest feelings.

"Just as I thought," he sighed.

"I love her," I confessed.

Since he had seen deep into my heart, there was no point trying to hide what was there.

"The thought of her drives me to madness. I love her so dearly. Please, please allow me to marry her."

"You must not," said the man in the tone of a venerable teacher. "I cannot allow it. Forget her."

"Is she promised to another man?"

"No."

"Am I not good enough for her?"

"I have no objection whatsoever on that score. You work hard and you have good business sense. I am sure you would be an excellent son-in-law."

"Then please may I ask why?"

Cornered by my questioning, the man hesitated. Then with a strange, sad look he said:

"Oyone is possessed by a fox."

Fox possession, as you know, is a mental abnormality involving the migration of a fox's spirit into a human. According to psychologists, it is a kind of psychosis, brought on by invocation.

I was dumbfounded by the father's words.

"So please," he said, "forget her."

"B…but," I stammered. "I've seen her many times. There's nothing odd about her at all. She is graceful and cheerful. She is entirely perfect."

"I'm afraid that's not true," the man said calmly. "She's possessed by a fox. I'm her father, and since my wife died young, I've been a mother to her too. Believe what I say."

"I cannot believe it," I shouted, bowing my head to the ground and stretching my hands out to his knees. "And I would not give up, even if what you said was true. My love will drive the fox out of her."

"That is impossible. It's no ordinary fox. And…" The man's tone suddenly darkened. "She is more than possessed."

"More than possessed?"

"I cannot speak of it." The man seemed to shrink physically, his back bent low as though bearing a huge, heavy yet invisible burden.

His white side-locks quivered in the cool autumnal afternoon wind. Despite our different ages, I suddenly felt a kind of affinity with him – a fellowship, man to man.

"Whether she's possessed, or whether she's more than possessed, I love your daughter and I am sure that I can make her happy. Please let me marry her."

The man looked up and stared into my eyes. He smiled weakly.

"In that case you had better see her true self with your own eyes. Stay here tonight. Sleep in the room next to hers. See for yourself what happens. I tell you: in the morning you will crawl out of here and never come near the place again. I won't stop you going, of course, but I would ask one thing of you – you can run off, but don't tell anyone else of what you see or hear tonight."

The three of us had supper together that evening. Oyone was delightful. She looked after me wonderfully. She filled my *sake* cup whenever it was empty. If there was the faintest sound of a mosquito she fanned the air to drive it away.

"How on earth could such a kind girl be possessed by a fox?" I said to myself as I lay down on the futon that had been prepared for me. The *sake* soon took me off into a deep sleep.

I am not sure how long I had been asleep before I was awoken by the sound of someone sobbing. I listened carefully and realised that it came from Oyone's room next door. "What is she crying about at this time of night?" I wondered.

I climbed out of my mosquito net and put my ear to the sliding screen that separated her room from mine. As I listened I began to think the sobbing might equally be a kind of laughter. Then I heard a sound like that of a cat lapping water. My knees trembled. My spine shivered.

"Perhaps it is as her father says," I thought. "She *is* possessed by a fox but she only becomes like that deep in the night, when even the autumn insects are silent and asleep."

In other circumstances I would have hidden my head in my futon and lain there trembling until the light of morning. But I loved Oyone and I wanted to see her true self, as her father had suggested. I slid the screen open one centimetre.

Inside Oyone's mosquito net was a fox – a large fox, with a back as long as a human's. Its fur was white. The fox's body was between Oyone's open thighs, its loins thrusting forward and back, forward and back. What I had heard of course was not Oyone crying; it was voracious moans of delight. The cat lapping water requires no explanation.

The movements of the fox and Oyone became frenzied. Then suddenly they stopped. The fox said something quietly to Oyone in a high-pitched voice, and then crawled out of the mosquito net. It put on a *yukata* robe that was lying on the floor, and sat down cross-legged, looking extremely self-satisfied. It took a pipe from a pouch, filled it with tobacco, struck a match, and started to smoke.

"This is a dream," I thought. "It must be!"

I rubbed my eyes repeatedly, but the pipe-smoking fox did not disappear.

Then I noticed the faint smell of tobacco.

"It's no dream if I can smell the tobacco!" I thought.

I had not the courage to look any longer at the nightmarish spectacle in Oyone's room. I closed the screen and lay down quietly in my futon, but I did not sleep at all for the rest of the night.

In the morning I went to her father's room.

"Did you see it?" he asked quietly.

I nodded.

"So you will forget about her," he said.

I shook my head. "I don't give up so easily," I said.

"What do you mean?" he said. "Are you mad? That animal is the spirit of the shrine behind the house. It's not just a fox. It's a kind of god. It's far too strong to fight against."

"A *god*?" I exclaimed angrily shaking my fist in the man's face. "Gods don't sit cross-legged and smoke pipes! They don't lounge around in *yukata* looking smug! That's just an old fox! I'm going to get rid of it. And once that's done, Oyone will be back to normal!"

"B-but," stammered the man. "How on earth are you going to get rid of it?"

"I thought of a plan while I was lying awake before dawn," I said. "I'm going to teach the fox a lesson. May I stay here one more night?"

The man thought for a long while and then nodded.'

Inubuse picked up some tongs and wrote a character in the ashes of the hearth. I leaned forward to see what he had written: 針 – needle.

'My plan was to put needles in the fox's *yukata*.'

He raked over the character.

'I thought that if I put thirty or so needles in the *yukata* one or two of them would prick the fox's skin. I borrowed a *yukata*, took it down to the riverbed and carefully concealed the needles in it. If I had done so at the house, of course, it might have been noticed by the fox of the shrine.

Night came. As soon as Oyone went to bed, I took the *yukata* and hid under the veranda outside her room. I would swap the garments whilst Oyone and the fox were busy. It was risky, but it was the best I could think of. I waited, enduring the merciless attacks of mosquitoes. Suddenly the insects fell quiet.

"He's come!" I thought.

I looked out into the darkness. There was a padding sound. A vague white figure came into view.

"That's him!"

He was wearing a short *yukata*, his furry white tail visible below the hem. I stayed stock still, and held my breath. The white figure stopped right in front of me and then jumped lightly up on to the veranda above. I breathed quietly several times and then lifted my head above the veranda floor. The fox was outside the mosquito net, looking down at Oyone as she lay inside. She was fast asleep.

With a shake of his shoulders the fox slipped off his *yukata* and went inside the net. He stood over Oyone. She started to murmur. Then – more horrific to me than the noise of the guardians of hell sharpening their swords – the lapping sound began.

"Now's my chance!" I thought. "He's lost to the world, and he's got his back to me..."

I crawled up onto the veranda. Stretching my arm out, I pulled the fox's *yukata* towards me and replaced it with the one in which I had concealed the needles. By the time I was back under the veranda the fox had stopped moving.

"Come on, you bastard," I thought. "Put it on!" The wait was unbearable.

"Ahh!" cried a voice and something white shot past me into the garden. In an instant the white figure of the old fox merged into the darkness of the night and could be seen no more.

As I crawled out from under the veranda my hand slipped on the wet surface of the stone step. I lifted my hand to my nose. It smelled of blood. Oyone was fast asleep inside the mosquito net.'

Inubuse put his hand to his nose as though recalling that smell of blood. Then he suddenly frowned.

'What happened next?' I asked.

'Everything seemed to have gone very well. The fox didn't return.'

'Would it really be put off by a couple of needle pricks?' I said.

'I dipped the needles in wolfsbane,' said Inubuse.

'...'

'Her father agreed to our marriage and we settled in a rented house in Kamaishi. I didn't want to stay at her father's house, as I thought that, with the shrine in the garden, the fox might reappear.'

'Did you think nothing of...' I hesitated.

'Of what?' said Inubuse.

'I am sorry to ask this, but Oyone did have this special relationship with a fox. Didn't you wonder about that at all?'

'It worried me a little. But then, Oyone had known nothing about it – she had been forced to give her body unconsciously whilst under the fox's spell. So I just chased the thought of their abominable relationship from my mind.'

He smoked his pipe in silence for a while.

Eventually Inubuse wearily resumed his tale.

'Nothing special happened for a time. We were happy.'

His voice sounded quite the opposite.

'My work was going well. Within a year I had established my own small tailoring business. Oyone was playing a vital role in its success.

"Take some brown Oshima to Mr ABC in Tono tomorrow," she would suddenly murmur. I'd go there, and sure enough, he would buy several hundred yen's worth just like that. Oyone always knew who was going to marry whom, when and where. "Miss EFG from Ozuchi is to marry in six months," she once said. "Take a set of bridal clothes over. If you don't go tomorrow, someone else will get in before you." I was dubious about it, but went anyway. When I arrived, the EFGs were astonished. "How do you know about the wedding? We haven't told anyone yet. We were just about to tell the relatives." They were so impressed that they ordered a complete bridal outfit.

I don't know where Oyone got the information but it was always reliable. Strangely, she only gave it when we were making love. So to get as much information as I could, I made love to her every night.

While this was going on, I noticed something uncanny. On those occasions when she gave me really excellent information, it felt as though she was not with me at all. I mean, physically she was in my arms, but it seemed as though in a deeper sense she was with somebody else.

One day in late autumn the year after our wedding I decided to take Oyone to a nearby hot spring. Our business was established and new customers were coming to us every day. We had nothing to worry about. So I wanted to give my wife a treat, some relaxation after a year's hard work. But on our way through the mountains, something terrible happened.

With just a few kilometres further to walk, a shiba dog appeared on the path ahead of us. Oyone suddenly grew pale and began to tremble.

"What's the matter?" I said, taking her hand. "The dog's all right. It isn't wild. It looks like a well-trained hunting dog. Good hunting dogs don't bite people. Don't be afraid."

But Oyone's fear grew. Her trembling became violent. The dog was now barking. The barking grew fiercer and fiercer, until Oyone, unable to stand it anymore, shook her hand free and ran off into the wood to the left of the road. The dog ran swiftly after her.

"Oyone! Come back!" I shouted. "If you run, the dog will get even more worked up!"

But it was no use. My voice vanished into the deep red of the autumn forest. Oyone didn't come back. I sat down at the side of the road with my pipe to wait. Just then I heard a loud noise deep in the forest – like wooden clappers. I stood up in surprise and looked amongst the trees. I could hear the sound of rustling undergrowth. Eventually a hunter emerged from the forest, accompanied by the shiba dog. On the hunter's back was an iron trap. In the trap was a large fine-coated vixen caught by her front paw. She was still struggling.

"Foxes are clever creatures," the hunter said. "If they're caught in one of these traps they'll chew up their own leg to get free. But this one didn't have time. I happened to be just there when she ran into the trap. She's unlucky, I suppose."'

Bang! Bang! Bang! The sound of more fireworks reached the cave. I glanced at my watch and saw that it was past one o'clock – time I was back at the sanatorium.

'So Oyone wasn't *possessed* by a fox, after all,' I said. 'She actually *was* a fox, wasn't she?'

Inubuse didn't reply.

'Your wife was a fox, and after you married she continued to have her relationship with the white fox from the shrine at Arakane – through your body. That's what happened, isn't it? The white fox felt sorry for you, and to make amends gave you all that information, through Oyone. That was it, wasn't it?'

Inubuse rubbed his hand round and round his scalp.

'Perhaps it was – perhaps it wasn't,' he said. 'Perhaps Oyone disappeared. The fox in the trap might have been nothing to do with her.'

'But…'

'Since then I have lived alone. When I reported Oyone's disappearance to her father he simply nodded and said "I see." As I told you, he had become very rich after finding a gold deposit in the mountains. One rumour was that it had actually been his wife who had found the gold. Who knows – maybe the same thing happened to him as to me.'

Inubuse slowly poured some barley tea into his cup and I stood up to leave. The sound of another daytime firework reached the cave.

話売り
Story Seller

The sanatorium was a melancholy place. Long ago people abandoned old relatives in the mountains; here they abandoned their sick. After a patient had been admitted, the family didn't often visit. The sanatorium was difficult to get to of course, but I don't think that was the only reason. I sometimes sensed the flicker of a cruel smile as people left a patient behind. 'That's that problem sorted out,' they seemed to be thinking. So I felt depressed whenever new patients arrived.

My main job at the sanatorium was to calculate monthly pay for the staff – doctors, nurses, kitchen staff, and so on. This work was easily completed in three days, so the remaining twenty-seven days of the month were spent propping myself up on the desk waiting for lunchtime. When lunchtime came I would be able to listen to one of Inubuse's stories – my only enjoyment in those days.

I wonder how many stories I heard from Inubuse in all. I was at the sanatorium for about two-and-a-half years, so it must have been at least five or six hundred. If each cost a thousand yen, then in total they would be worth five or six hundred thousand. I am sorry to start on this mercenary note, but I do have a reason. Inubuse once told me that until about 1935 there were people in the region who made their living by selling stories. I've just remembered his story about a 'story seller,' so I think I'll sell that story on to you.

'I haven't been lucky with marriage,' said Inubuse. 'I've had three wives. First, I married a girl in Tokyo, then Oyone. And the third was a woman called Okinu…'

I forget the exact date, but it was getting cold – the first serious snows of winter were not far off. I had rushed into the cave and was warming my hands by the hearth. Inubuse was at the back of the cave, rifling through a wicker trunk.

'Getting married three times sounds good to me,' I said. In those days I dreamed of touching every woman in the world. My philosophy was quantity rather than quality. Or, to put it another way, I was adolescent.

The old man found a sleeveless cotton-padded jacket from the bottom of the trunk, and, pulling it over his shoulders, came back to the hearth.

'Nobody gets together with someone they dislike,' he said, as if talking to himself. 'People get together because they love each other. So it's tough when you part. I've been through it three times. That proves how unlucky I've been.'

As he talked he was carefully picking loose threads off the padded jacket. The jacket looked as though it had been washed many times. It was faded, its hem was torn, and cotton padding was coming out.

'This jacket was made by my third wife. I met her at a drinking place in Kamaishi.'

'A drinking place?'

'Yes,' he said. 'A special type of drinking place. There was one room downstairs, and two upstairs. You drank downstairs and then went upstairs with a woman if you wanted to.'

'You mean it was a brothel?'

'That's right. There was a whole row of them down by the shore. My third wife worked in one of those.'

'So you mean…' I couldn't bring myself to say it.

'Well, yes. She was a prostitute.' The old man said it for me, with no hesitation.

'After Oyone went, I kept my tailor's shop in Kamaishi. But without her, the business didn't go well. I started drinking heavily in those bars.

There were different ways into that part of town. One was via the main street and the other was across a rank area of waste ground. The waste ground was used year-round for drying fish for fertiliser, and in one corner was a pool of effluent from the iron works. The stench made your eyes water.

It was about this time of year – the start of winter. The sun was going down and there was an icy wind. I was crossing the waste ground towards the bars when I heard voices behind a pile of fertiliser sacks. For no particular reason I stopped and listened.

"So you have to run away then!"

It was a child's voice, full of sorrow. I quietly moved around the sacks to find a young woman stroking a little girl's hands. The girl was crying uncontrollably. Looking carefully, I saw that her hands were badly swollen. She seemed to have a serious case of chilblains. The swelling would go down, but the skin would never recover completely. I had suffered from chilblains as a child, so I wanted to help.

"Put some grated radish in hot water," I said, "and soak her hands for fifteen minutes. She'll feel much better."

The young woman looked at me in surprise. Her body was thin as wire, but her face was pleasant. Her eyes were large and wet with tears. They were beautiful eyes.

"By the way," I said, "I heard talk about running away. You're lucky it was only me that heard. You could be in trouble if someone else had."

There was a rumour that women who absconded from the brothels had their fingers broken. The brothel owners didn't want to damage the women's faces or bodies as these were stock in trade. So they broke the third and fourth fingers of the left hand. To ensure it would be a deterrent, the other women were made to watch. I hadn't witnessed it myself, so for me it was just a rumour. But I had seen a number of women in the area with loose fingers, so I think it was true.

"My father's ill," said the young woman desperately. "It's very serious. He may die tomorrow, but according to my sister he sometimes opens his eyes wide and speaks. He says he's given up on life, but that before he dies he wants to see my face, if only for a moment." She began to sob. "He wants to apologise to me."

I guessed that what troubled him as he faced death was that his poverty had led him to sell his daughter into prostitution. He felt he couldn't die without apologising to her. Of course, his poverty wouldn't have been his fault. There had been years of bad harvests in the Sanriku district, and though they worked like cattle, many poor farmers had been unable to survive without selling their daughters. But this man wished to apologise to the daughter he had sold, blaming himself entirely. It was a pitiful situation.

"Go and see your father," I said. "I'll pay your employer the money you'd have earned while you are away."

That was how I met her. I started to frequent the place where she worked. Six months later I paid off her debts and she was free. We started living together. Her name was Okinu.

Although I managed to pay off Okinu's debts, I did so with borrowed money, which I had to pay back as quickly as possible. I didn't think I could earn that amount easily through my tailoring business, so I decided the time had come to change my line of work. Through an acquaintance, I got a job as a pack-horse driver at a wholesaler in Ozuchi, the fishing port between Kamaishi and Miyako.'

'Do pack-horse drivers earn that much money?' I asked.

'It was quite a good business in those days. For example, a driver would start out from Ozuchi to Tono with fish in the evening (people think fish are transported in the morning when they are landed, but if they were they'd go off in the heat of the day; so they're kept at the market until the evening). So a driver would load up in the evening in Ozuchi and take the fish to Tono overnight via Fuefuki Pass. He'd arrive the next morning and the fish would be offloaded at the wholesaler. Then the horses would be loaded up again with rice and vegetables and he'd be back in Ozuchi late in the afternoon. For a return trip he'd get eighteen litres of rice per horse. Of course, nobody ever took just one horse. A driver worth his salt would take five or six horses. With five horses he'd get ninety litres of rice – more than a whole sack. So he'd earn enough rice for a month with just one return trip to Tono. That's good business.

Anyway, we rented a small house on the outskirts of Ozuchi, and I travelled to Tono every other day. Within three months I repaid the money I'd borrowed for Okinu's release. After another three months, we bought the house we'd been renting. In the meantime Okinu had been gradually recovering from her life of degradation. She had blossomed into a really attractive woman – almost unrecognisable. When she had been very thin, her large eyes had protruded in a rather odd way; but now she had put on weight they looked more settled, and I have to say, seductive. Her bust was now ample and voluptuous. She was at the peak of womanhood. As a consequence people began to talk about her. "Inubuse's missus," they said, "is a cracker."

But she wasn't just beautiful. She began to learn needlework, and in three months was as skilled as any seamstress. She made this jacket. An ordinary seamstress would have taken a day to make it; she finished it in a morning. She was a marvel in the kitchen too, chopping, slicing, trimming, filleting – all with a single knife. And to top everything she had a very kind heart. Not a day went by without me thinking what a wonderful wife I had.

My work was well-paid, but tough. Walking all night, and then all the next day, was exhausting. And Fuefuki Pass was a dangerous place. Wild dogs lived there. They looked just like ordinary dogs, but they were fiercer than wolves. I often encountered whole packs of them, especially on the way from Ozuchi to Tono. It was hardly surprising really, considering the amount of fish the horses were carrying.

To keep the dogs away, I took to ringing a loud bell as I crossed the pass. Sometimes as I was clanging my own bell I would hear another bell in the distance. The faint sound of another bell was very comforting – it meant that somewhere in the pass I had a comrade.'

Inubuse relit his pipe and smoked for a while. I took the opportunity to pour some hot water into the teapot and make some tea. He took a mouthful, then tapping the edge of the hearth with his pipe, resumed the story.

'It was my first summer as a pack-horse driver. One night I was climbing up through Fuefuki Pass, clanging my bell as always to keep the dogs away, when I noticed a small light ahead of me, a bright blur in the pitch-black starless, moonless night. I thought for a moment that it might be a firefly, but, no, it didn't seem quite like that. I felt uneasy, but a pack-horse driver couldn't turn back just because of nerves. There was nothing for it but to push straight on. So ringing my bell more vigorously than ever, I continued walking towards the strange, small light.

I smiled at myself when I eventually realised what it was. It seemed absurd – the light was tobacco. An old man with a rough beard was smoking a cigar stub stuffed into a pipe. I was very relieved and decided to have a smoke there myself. Unfastening the tobacco pouch from my waist I walked towards the man.

"Would you give me a light?" I said. "Of course I've some matches myself, but…"

The old man didn't wait for me to finish.

"Are you going to buy a story?" he said.

"Ah hah!" I thought. "This man must be a story seller." I had heard that along the Sanriku coast there were four or five story sellers – people who went from one village to the next picking up gossip and selling it on, hearing stories and repeating them for money.

"I've got one saved up for you, pack-horse driver. How about it?"

As I said before, the money was good with my new job, and I was well-off. I didn't know how much a story would be, but I thought it must be less than a yen. I decided to buy a story just for fun.

"I don't mind buying one," I said. "But I'm not going to pay a lot for it. No more than fifty sen."

The story seller tugged his beard and thought for a while.

"All right," he said. "Fifty sen."

He made himself comfortable and then he spoke.

"I'm going to sell you the following story. Ready? Once upon a time in a field there was a big tree and a little tree."

I listened intently.

"One day, for some reason, the big tree fell over while the little tree stayed just as it was. And that is all. Rata-tat-tat."

"Is that the end?"

"Yes, that's the end. Shall I take my fifty sen now?"

"That's ridiculous," I muttered reaching for the purse around my neck. "It's a kind of fraud."

I took out a fifty-sen coin and passed it to the old man.

"You've taught me a lesson!" I said. "I'll not to be tempted to buy a story again."

"I wonder if that's true," said the story seller, tugging his beard.

He stood up and suddenly walked off in the direction of Ozuchi.'

'What a funny old man!' I said laughing. 'He really took you in, didn't he?'

Inubuse ignored me and carried on with his story. His earnest tone silenced my laughter.

'About two weeks later, I was approaching the outskirts of Ozuchi, the horses laden with aubergines and cucumbers. The sky, which until then had been clear blue, suddenly darkened. I looked upwards with foreboding. Black clouds were racing across from west to east. The sky was like a basin suddenly awash with ink. I must get on, I thought. But hailstones, the size of small pebbles, had already begun to fall. I looked around at the empty landscape. There was nothing but the road and fields. The only prospects of shelter were two *keyaki* trees, one large one small, a hundred metres further down the road. I decided to shelter from the hail under the larger tree, and ran towards it with the horses. There was a flash of lightning overhead and a roll of thunder. I ran and ran and at last reached the tree. As I was catching my breath, I suddenly remembered the story I had bought that night at the Fuefuki Pass.

"…the big tree fell over while the little tree stayed just as it was."

I ran out from under the large tree and hurried the horses to shelter under the small tree, twenty metres away. A great sheet of lightning tore through the sky, and with a tremendous crash of thunder I was thrown to the ground. For a while I lay motionless. Then, summoning the courage to look up, I glanced fearfully over to the large *keaki* tree and saw nothing but a charred stump. That fifty sen had saved my life.

After that I always looked out for the story seller when I went through Fuefuki Pass. I was greatly in his debt and I wanted to thank him. In fact, I also wanted to get another story from him.'

'And did you see him?' I asked.

'Well, time went by and autumn came. The pass turned a wonderful red. One day I bought some *sake* at a shop in Tono before leaving. When I was near the pass I tied the horses to a tree and sat down with my flask to admire the colours of the leaves. As I was sipping the *sake*, I heard a voice behind me.

"Hey pack-horse driver! Would you give me a drop of *sake*?"

I looked around and there was the story seller leaning on a stick.

"How was that story you bought for fifty sen?" he said. "Was it good?"

"Good?" I said, running over to him and clasping his wrinkled hand. "It was the most useful story I've ever heard! Don't just ask for a drop! You must have the whole flask!"

As if he had been my own aged father, I prepared a place for him on the grass, poured him some *sake* and placed some dried squid in his palm. The old man slurped the *sake* contentedly for a while and then, as though remembering something, said:

"You still seem to be doing well."

"Not bad," I said.

"Not bad…" he echoed.

"But I have my worries… they don't go away…" I said

"Would those worries be about your wife?" he said.

The old man guessed right. Okinu was a rare find. She was kind, she was good at sewing and cooking, but what's more, she had that "something" about her which really attracted men. I'd heard a lot of remarks about her.

"Oh, what I'd give for one night with Inubuse's wife!"

"Maybe I'll slip in and see her when her husband's away."

"Now *there's* a body to set your juices running. I saw her washing the other day…"

"They say she was a whore in Kamaishi. A leopard doesn't change its spots, you know. She'd probably give us the goods if we paid."

I'd heard that kind of banter at the bathhouse, at the barber, out drinking. The men would talk loudly, not thinking I was there. Hearing remarks like that, I gradually grew to hate my job. Driving the pack-horses meant being away every other night. What would I do if what the men said in their jokes actually happened?

"So you *are* worried about your wife then," the old man grinned. "In that case, why not buy another story? This one concerns your wife."

"Yes! Yes please!" I said and pressed my purse into the old man's hand. "There's about twenty-five yen in there. Take it all."

The old man opened the purse and took out one fifty-sen coin.

"Fifty sen is enough," he said. "Are you ready?" he asked. "This is today's story. Once upon a time there was a happy couple. The couple always said, 'Only suspect when you've asked a hundred times.' They repeated it every day, like a prayer. The End. Rata-tat-tat."

When he had finished his story the old man stood up and gave me back my purse. He then walked off, as fast as the wind, in the direction of Tono.

That day I arrived back in Ozuchi after sunset. I was later than usual because of the time I had spent at the pass. I left the horses at the warehouse and walked slowly home, thinking about the local men's banter.

"I wasn't at home last night," I thought. "If people see I'm not there today either, they may get ideas. I shouldn't leave poor Okinu alone. I must get back to her as quickly as I can."

So I began to walk fast. When I arrived outside the house I was astonished to see a figure through the opaque glass of the tea room – it was the figure of a man. Blood rushed to my head and I picked up a heavy piece of firewood from the pile under the eave. But then I thought "Wait!" I remembered the story I'd just heard. "Only suspect when you've asked a hundred times." I had only seen the figure through opaque glass, and then just for a moment. I couldn't be sure it was a man. I went to the front door, opened it quickly, and looked carefully around.

"Hello!" said my wife, skipping towards me from the tea room. "You must be tired. Will you go to the bathhouse now? Or would you like something to drink?"

"Give me some *sake*!" I said.

"Of course!" she said.

"Wait!" I said. "I want to ask you something first."

Okinu looked up at me with glistening eyes.

"I think someone was sitting in the tea room just now. Am I right?"

"Yes," she said "I was there." She gazed at me wide-eyed as if to say, "What is the matter? Why are you angry?"

Nothing more happened that day, but the following afternoon, as I was on my way to the warehouse, my suspicions began to grow again. Perhaps that figure the previous evening *had* been a man, after all. The nearer I got to the warehouse the stronger my suspicions became. I decided to find out the truth. I couldn't walk all the way to Tono with this doubt needling at my mind.

"Okinu will think I'm leaving for Tono late this afternoon, as usual," I thought. "If she's got a man, she's sure to have him over tonight. I'm going to catch him."

I told the warehouse that I would have to set off later than normal that day, and then I went to the harbour wall to pass the time until it was dark. When I thought the time was right I set off back home. As I approached the house I looked towards the opaque glass and sank down in despair. There were two figures behind the glass – Okinu's and a man's.

"It's just the right temperature, darling."

Okinu's voice came through the glass as her figure offered *sake* to the figure of the man. There was no doubt now – she had a man. Somewhere in my head the story seller was shouting, "Only doubt when you have asked a hundred times." But with a situation as clear as this, why ask anybody anything?

"You whore!" I shouted, kicking down the opaque glass door and bursting into the room.

Okinu gaped at me, still holding the *sake* flask. The man was facing the other way, unable to move.

"How could you betray me?" I shouted, kicking her. She fell slowly backwards towards the brazier, still with the *sake* in her hands.'

'…What a nasty woman,' I muttered. 'She utterly betrayed you.'

Inubuse shook his head sadly.

'No, she didn't. No woman could have had a kinder heart. The truth is that what I thought was her lover was actually a straw dummy. She'd made it herself.'

'A straw dummy?'

'Yes. She had dressed it in my kimono and was pretending to serve it *sake*.'

'Why would she do a thing like that…?'

'To say to the local men – My husband is here with me. He won't put up with any of your tricks, so keep away.'

'…'

'I think another reason was that she was terribly lonely while I was gone.'

'What happened to her?'

'When she fell, she hit her head hard on the edge of the brazier and died. Basically, I'd killed her.'

We sat for a long time in silence. Eventually Inubuse opened his mouth and said simply:

'People have to be able to trust each other. Without that, everything falls apart.'

沼
Lake

'Do you know Lake Jimbe?' Inubuse asked one lunchtime as I arrived at his cave. It was my second spring at the government sanatorium near Kamaishi. 'It's in the next valley but one to the south of here.'

I nodded as I sat down by the hearth. Lake Jimbe is a small lake, about a hundred metres across. I had been there twice to look for lily roots. It had seemed an eerie place. On both occasions it had been covered in a thin mist, and the water had been green, presumably because of weed growing below the surface.

'They say it's called Jimbe after an old man who lived by the lake, digging lily roots for his living. The incident I'm going to talk about happened by the lake.'

I was intrigued by the word 'incident.' I wondered what Inubuse meant.

'But to say the incident *happened* by the lake is not entirely accurate. Perhaps I should say that it *ended* by the lake. The incident originated at the Nakahashi Mine, over the next mountain to the south of the lake. Have you been there?'

I shook my head. The Nakahashi Mine was no longer in use and the mountain between the lake and the mine was about five hundred metres high so you couldn't easily get from one to the other. Anybody curious to see the site of the Nakahashi Mine (assuming anybody would have such a worthy interest) would have approached from Kamaishi on the coast. I think there was a bus five times a day.

'The Nakahashi Mine,' said Inubuse, 'was an iron ore mine operating from the late days of the Meiji Period until 1945, when its deposits were exhausted. It was a small concern, with just one pithead. Unlike most mines near here it wasn't owned by Kamaishi Iron or any other large company. It was owned by a rich local man called Tsuda. It had been clear from the very start that deposits were limited so Tsuda had never invested in equipment. The miners went up and down to the face fifty metres below by ladder. The "ladders" were just tree trunks with pieces of pole banged in to the sides with long nails. They were extremely dangerous. Those in greatest peril were not the men who worked at the face, but the men who carried the ore to the pithead. They crawled back and forth to the surface hundreds of times a day, carrying forty-kilo loads of ore in baskets made of hemp and bamboo. If someone near the top missed his footing on the tree-trunk ladder there'd be a disaster – everyone below would fall with him. In 1935 there were about a hundred men working at the mine. Some seventy per cent were Korean and the rest Japanese. The Japanese were all strange individuals with dark pasts. I was relatively ordinary.'

'You mean you worked there?' I said.

'Yes,' he said, 'for about a year.'

He gave a deep sigh. He looked on the verge of tears.

'One year in that place was like a hundred years in hell. At five in the morning supervisors would wake us and herd us into the mine with long wooden batons. We came out again at ten at night. We didn't see the sun all year long.'

'Why did you have to work in a place like that?'

'I brought it on myself,' he smiled bitterly, putting some wood in the hearth.

'After my wife died I let myself go – drinking, fighting, gambling.'

He lifted the tousled, white-flecked hair from his forehead to reveal a deep scar running just below his hairline.

'Scars like this were part of life for me in those days. I made my living cheating people.'

'You mean you were a con man?'

Inubuse ignored me.

'In the end I was arrested by the police.'

He didn't seem to want to talk about the exact nature of his activities, so I didn't probe.

'I thought I'd go to court and be given six months or so in jail. But something happened behind the scenes – Tsuda, the owner of the mine, had an arrangement with the police. People arrested for assault, burglary, or fraud were employed by Tsuda as mine workers. Everybody was seen to benefit. For the criminals it meant avoiding prison. For Tsuda, it meant a cheap labour force who weren't going to disappear quickly if they didn't like the conditions. For the police, sending scum to the mines meant a contribution to the national policy of increasing production – it also meant they didn't have to look too deeply into the relevant cases.

But in fact, to say all sides benefited is nonsense. It was Tsuda and the police who benefited. We suffered. If I'd known how bad things were going to be, I'd gladly have gone to prison. But of course at the time it didn't occur to me that anything could be worse than prison. I was just relieved not to have a criminal record.

But as soon as I arrived at the mine, my relief vanished. They say that convicts sent to the gold mines of Sado Island in the Edo period lived on average only three years after they arrived. Well, the Sado mines must have been pretty much like ours. Our accommodation was worse than a stable. We slept on straw with tree trunks for pillows. When it rained we got soaked. When it was hot, we were attacked by flies and mosquitoes. In winter, there would be ten centimetres of snow on the straw every morning. Our tree-trunk pillows served as an ingenious type of alarm clock – a supervisor would hit the trunk with a thick stick at five in the morning, and however tired we were the thud would startle us awake. The diet was terrible. One helping of barley rice, a slice of pickled vegetable, and a cup of *kombu* soup. *Kombu* soup may sound nice, but it was just squashed *kombu* stalks. They were tough, indigestible, and tasted foul.'

The old man was silent for a while, looking at the fire in the hearth.

'But there was one thing worse than the work, the accommodation, and the diet – or should I say one man? One particular supervisor. There were ten supervisors in all – each of them vicious individuals, without feeling or mercy. But worst of the lot was Sawamatsu.'

Inubuse stopped again.

'He must have been very brutal,' I said, trying to encourage Inubuse to continue.

He nodded.

'Sawamatsu was inhuman. He had worked his way up from being a miner himself, and though "supervisor" wasn't much of a position, he didn't want to lose it. So he was always trying to look good in front of Tsuda, and that meant us suffering. He beat us and kicked us every day. If ore production fell, he withheld rations. That barley rice and scrap of pickled vegetable were all we had to enjoy in life. Being denied them was terrible. But we just had to clench our teeth and keep working.'

'Why didn't you run away?' I said. 'Was there no opportunity?'

'No. The miner who knew most about it was Sato. He'd been in the mine longer than anyone else.

"In my seven years here," he told me, "more than fifty people have tried to get away, but only one managed it – a man called Kaneda. Sawamatsu hated him. Kaneda asked to rest one day because he was ill. Sawamatsu got furious. He flogged him, and wrenched off the little finger of his right hand. Kaneda must have thought he was going to be killed, and a few days later he ran off. He's the only one out of fifty to get away. That's a very low success rate. If it was one in two, I'd have tried long ago."

If men were caught, they were flogged in front of the others and their rations were halved for a month. This scared me and kept me in that hellish place for almost a year.

Then, one day, when I was eating my barley rice ball at midday down the mine, part of the tunnel caved in. It wasn't a major collapse – the area affected was only one metre by five. It started quite slowly with a few fragments of rock, so I managed to jump out of the way with just a few cuts and bruises. When the cloud of dust settled I gasped in amazement. There was a beam of sunlight in the mine. Specks of dust were floating in the light.

I stood in the shaft of light and looked up. I could see the sun through a hole in the roof. I had spent a whole year like a mole, never seeing the sun. My eyes were dazzled. I sneezed.

I wondered how we could be so near the surface when the pit-head was fifty metres above the tunnel. It occurred to me that as the tunnel had lengthened, it had veered away from the mountain so that now we were some way across the valley from the mine entrance.

While I was thinking, three miners who had heard the crash arrived at the scene. One of them was Sato.

"This may be fate," he said as we gazed up. "We'll be able to get out if we make the hole a bit bigger. If we want to run for it, now's our chance."

He looked slowly at each of us. What were we going to do?

"If we don't act quick," he said, "a supervisor will be here on his rounds."

I took a step forward and looked up at the hole from a different angle I could see blue sky. That blue entranced me. If I could just have one day – half a day – out of this dark, dusty mine, if I could only walk under that blue sky, I would happily give up the rest of my life.

"I'm going," I said, finally uttering words that had stuck in my throat all year.

"You don't have to come with me, but if you stay, keep quiet for a while – for the sake of friendship."

I swung a pickaxe up at the edge of hole above. Earth tumbled in, doubling the size of the hole. It was now easily big enough to get through.

"Let's go!" said one of the others. Sato nodded.

"We'll give you a leg up," he said. "When you're out, pull us up."

They joined hands to form a base for me to stand on. I stepped up and reached for the edge of the hole.'

'And then?' I said, desperate to hear what happened next. 'Did all four of you escape?'

Inubuse gently shook his head.

'What happened after that was terrible,' he said.

As usual, as he reached the climax of the story, the old man stopped to light his pipe. I picked up the tongs and took out my frustration on the ashes in the hearth.

'In the world outside, it was late spring. There were patches of snow in the valley.'

As he resumed his story, I thrust the tongs down into the ashes and looked at his face.

'The sun was bright, the sky was blue. We saw the green of pines, the yellow of withered grass, the white of the lingering snow. For a moment we stood spellbound by the colours that Nature had created, at how beautifully they contrasted and combined. But this was no time to be savouring such wonders. As soon as the hole was found, a search party would be dispatched. We had to reach safety before then.

"I think we'd better go east," said Sato, after thinking for a while. "That way we'll reach Kamaishi. It's a busy port and we should be safe in the crowds. We might get taken on as boat crew at the fish market. Or we could make a straight run for Matsushima – there's a regular boat there from Kamaishi."

We agreed. Actually, I had wanted to go in the exact opposite direction – to Tono. But there was no time for discussion – it was best to go along with the first suggestion.

We immediately ran off eastwards. In front of us was a mountain; once we'd got to the top of that, we'd be looking down on Kamaishi. But before we had run ten metres, Sato, who was leading the way, fell flat on his face, and wooden clappers sounded out in every direction. He had fallen over a trip wire stretched between two bushes. He pressed his hands together in apology. Luckily, he didn't seem to be hurt, and he quickly got to his feet, but then his face suddenly grew pale.

"They're after us!" he said.

Sure enough, in the shadow of the mountain to the south we could make out figures running towards us – one… two… three.

"In that case," I suggested, "let's go in three different directions. That way we'll each have only one to shake off."

"Right!" said one of the men. "I'll go west – to Tono." And off he ran.

Of course, I had wanted to go to Tono, but there was no time to stop him and talk it through, so instead, with the sun behind me, I set off north.

"Good luck!" I shouted to the other two as they headed east, but I doubt my voice reached them.

Going north turned out to be a mistake, as the supervisor who came in pursuit was the savage and extremely agile Sawamatsu. It was a long time since I had run and I was weak from the poor diet. In front of me was a very steep five hundred-metre mountain, the highest in the area. Sawamatsu was closing on me all the time.

By the time I reached the top of the mountain he was almost close enough to touch me. We were running fast just beyond the summit when by chance I fell. Sawamatsu's momentum kept him running for some metres. In the brief seconds this lucky fall gave me, I decided to roll down the mountain. We were now on the north face – it was very steep and still covered with snow. Rolling might be quicker than running. That quick decision put me fifty metres ahead of Sawamatsu. But he didn't give up. He seemed intent on pursuing me until I was too exhausted to go on.

Further down the mountain, where the slope became gentler, I came to a forest of cedar trees. I ran panting through the forest until I found myself at the edge of a lake – Lake Jimbe.

"It's no use," I thought. "If I keep running, he'll get me sooner or later. I'll have to change tactics."

Close to exhaustion, I had a bizarre idea. I decided to hide myself by shinning up a tree.

I jumped up onto the trunk of a cedar tree on the edge of the lake and started to climb. I'd been up and down the tree-trunk ladders in the mine so often that climbing was easier for me than running. When my feet were on the second or third branch up, Sawamatsu reached the lake. He stood right under my tree and looked carefully around. I pressed myself tight against the trunk and held my breath. I then noticed that my image was distinctly reflected in the green water of the lake.

"If he notices that," I thought, "I'm done for. Please don't let him look!"

My prayer didn't seem to have been heard. Sawamatsu pointed at my reflection.

"You bastard!" he shouted. "Think you can hide there, do you?"

"Oh no!" I thought. "He's found me."

Or so I assumed; but what Sawamatsu did next was very strange. He threw off his jacket and his long boots and dived into the water, straight towards my reflection. The reflection was so clear that he thought I was hiding at the bottom of the lake. I suppose, like me, he was very tired.

"Whew!" I thought and slid down the tree. "Now I can gain some time!"

I picked up his boots and began to run through the forest again, keeping close to the lakeside.

"He'll find it tough running without his boots on this ground," I thought. "He'll hurt his feet so badly he won't even be able to walk."

But after I'd gone some way, I heard his voice closing in on me.

"You cheated me, you bastard!" he shouted. "And you stole my boots! I'll chase you to the end of the earth! I'm going to get you! Just wait!"

I'd clearly been quite wrong about the boots. His feet must have been very tough – he was running after me as fast as a deer.

When I was about halfway around the lake I noticed a hut among the cedars. Its walls and roof were entirely of bamboo grass.

"I'll hide in there," I thought.

I opened the bamboo-grass door to find a wild-looking man with long hair and beard. He was warming his hands by the bright red embers of the hearth. Above the fire was a kettle.

"I'm being chased," I said. "Please let me hide here!"

I knelt before him.

"Please!" I begged.

He stared at me.

"Who's chasing you?"

"A supervisor from Nakahashi Mine," I said. "A violent man called Sawamatsu. The Devil, we call him. He'll beat me 'til I'm half dead if he catches me."

"...The Devil, eh?"

He slowly stroked his beard. Then he tugged it, so that his head tilted forward in a nod.

"You can hide in a tea chest," he said, gesturing with his chin towards two tea chests at the back of the hut. "The smaller one, on the right."

I did as I was told. The chest seemed to be for clothes – it had two or three pieces of underwear in the bottom. I squatted down and down and bent forwards to fit inside. The man put the lid back on the chest. A few seconds later, I heard Sawamatsu's voice.

"A man came in here just now. Where are you hiding him?'

"I'm not hiding him. He came, but...'

"He came and...?'

"He hid in the lavatory outside."

"The bastard! I'll get him now. He's like a rat in a trap!"

"Wait!" called the man as Sawamatsu was about to dash outside. "There are no bushes around the lavatory. He'll notice you coming and run off. Why don't you hide in a tea chest instead?"

"You mean one of these?" Sawamatsu said.

"Yes... the larger one on the left."

I was astonished. What was the man going to do with me and Sawamatsu both in tea chests?

"I'll wait a while," the man said to Sawamatsu, "and then I'll tell him that you've given up and gone home."

"And then what?"

"Then I'll bring him in here to the hearth and give him some *sake*. When he's a little drunk and off his guard, you'll be able to get him."

"That's a good idea," said Sawamatsu.

His voice was just beside me. Then I heard the sound of someone opening the other tea chest and climbing in.

"That's it! I'm in," said Sawamatsu.

"I'll put the lid on," said the man.

"Wait!" said Sawamatsu.

"What is it?" said the man.

"Why are you helping me?" asked Sawamatsu. The man laughed softly.

"Well," he said, "I think I've had the honour of meeting you somewhere before."

"Oh? I don't remember that," said Sawamatsu.

"Oh well," said the man, "it doesn't matter. I'm going to put the lid on now, so duck your head."

I heard the lid being put firmly in place, and, after that, silence.

Suddenly I sensed brightness. The lid of my chest had been removed. I looked up and saw the man standing with his forefinger to his lips. I climbed quietly out of the chest. The man fetched some hemp string from a shelf.

He gestured that we should tie the other tea chest up with the string. I nodded and helped him.

"Hey! What are you doing?" said Sawamatsu as we passed the string under the bottom of the chest. "Why is the chest shaking?"

"I'm moving it into the corner so the man in the lavatory doesn't get suspicious about what's inside."

"I see."

Once we had tied the string securely around the chest, the man went over to the hearth and took out some red-hot tongs from among the embers.

"Ah! Now I remember! Mr Sawamatsu!" he said as he pressed the hot tongs against the tea chest. There was the smell of burning and a hole appeared in the chest.

"You're Sawamatsu, the supervisor from Nakahashi Mine, aren't you?"

"Yes, that's me. But why have you made this hole?"

The man rotated the tongs, making the hole bigger.

"It's a breathing hole, of course," he said.

"Oh," said Sawamatsu. "You're being very considerate."

"Well, you looked after me so well – at Nakahashi Mine."

"What?"

The man took the kettle from the hook above the hearth and held it over the hole in the tea chest.

"You were kind enough to flog me," he said cheerfully. "And thanks to you I lost the little finger of my right hand."

Sure enough there was no little finger on the hand that held the kettle. This must be Kaneda, I thought, the man who Sato had told me about – the only one who had succeeded in escaping from the Nakahashi Mine.

"Hey!" shouted Sawamatsu, battering at the lid of the tea chest. "What's going on? Open the lid! Open it!"

"I don't think that's nice now, is it?" said the man. "Imagine snapping off someone's precious little finger and not remembering! I don't feel much inclined to listen to the wishes of someone like that!"

"It can't be…" said Sawamatsu.

The movement inside the chest stopped for an instant before he spoke again. "Are you Kaneda…?"

"That's right," said the man. "Thank you for remembering."

"And you've been here all the time?"

"Yes. I make my living digging lily roots and selling them to restaurants. Well now, I think it's time to say bye-bye."

Kaneda slowly began to tip the kettle…'

Inubuse stopped speaking.

'Sawamatsu was killed wasn't he?' I said. 'Kaneda killed him, didn't he?"

Inubuse didn't answer.

'Oh! It's past one o'clock!' he said instead. 'You'd better be getting back.'

As I stood up to leave I wondered whether Inubuse might have helped Kaneda kill Sawamatsu. Perhaps that was why he left the story vague at the end.

This idea dominated my thoughts for some time.

鰻
Eel

'What's this?' asked Inubuse one noon in early summer. I had just arrived at the cave and passed him a small lunch box. 'It looks like *sekihan*.'

'That's right,' I nodded, sitting down by the hearth with my back to the mouth of the cave. 'Today is the sanatorium's second anniversary. All the staff were given *sekihan* to celebrate. Please have it.'

'But it's yours.'

'I've got another,' I said, pulling an identical box of the special rice from my jacket pocket. 'I got an extra from my friend in the kitchen.'

'Well, in that case.'

The old man opened the box and began to lick off grains of rice stuck to the inside of the lid.

He looked across at me.

'I've just remembered something – a very strange matter concerning *sekihan*. It happened thirty years ago.'

'Thirty years ago? That would be in the Taisho period, wouldn't it?'

I worked in the government sanatorium in the mountains near the Iwate coast from 1953 to 1954, so thirty years before would have been around 1923, towards the end of the reign of Emperor Taisho.

'Fifteen kilometres west of here, towards Tono,' Inubuse said, 'there's a village called Saoda. Do you know it?'

He picked up an *azuki* bean with his chopsticks and flicked it into his mouth.

I nodded. I had been to Saoda two or three times chasing up payments for medical charges. It had struck me as a lifeless and depressing village.

'It was a thriving place before the war,' he said. 'They had a large iron ore mine.'

He put the lid back on his box of *sekihan*. He'd obviously decided to tell his story before having lunch. I put my own box to one side. The story was bound to be better than a box of *sekihan*.

'I was working as a book-keeper at the mine,' he said. 'It was a very boring job – writing up figures, day in day out.'

'I know what you mean,' I said. 'That's just what I do at the moment.'

'Near the pit was a shrine called the Matsuo Shrine. It had festivals twice a year, in early summer and late autumn, and on those days the mine would close. There would be a circus near the mine offices, balladeers in the school hall, and rows of food stalls and amusements around the shrine. And we would each be given a box of *sekihan* and a bottle of *sake*. Some of the staff were expert flute-players and drummers, and they would spend the day performing. Some would sneak in and listen to the balladeers. Others would ignore the festival altogether. They would go whoring in Kamaishi or Tono, or go up onto the hills behind the mine to lie about on the grass doing nothing.'

'What did you do?'

'I went to the hills and drank *sake* with colleagues. We were up there on the day of the summer festival one year when somebody said:

"There's a pond over there. Why don't we go in and try to catch some fish. There's not much point sitting around drinking all day."

We were bored so most of us welcomed the idea and immediately began to take off our clothes. One person objected, however. He was a long-serving member of the accounts section, a man with a face so remarkably devoid of characteristics that he resembled an eel. So that was what we called him – Eel.

"I'm serious," Eel said vehemently. "Don't go into the pond. It may not look very big, but it's bottomless. A number of people have lost their lives there."

"There's no such thing as a bottomless pond," we said. "Maybe over the years there have been one or two people who've got stuck in the mud and drowned, but we don't have to worry about that. We can put ropes around ourselves and tie one end to a tree on the bank. Then if someone gets into trouble, the others can pull him to safety. As long as we take precautions, there'll be no problem."

But Eel kept his ground, and in the end he said, "If you catch the fish in that pond, the village will suffer great misfortune. In the 1780s there was a famine in this area and hungry farmers drained the pond to take the fish. Immediately afterwards there was a dysentery epidemic and within three days most of the villagers were dead. The guardian spirit of the pond had been angered and cursed the village."

"The guardian of the pond?" we said. "Who would that be?"

"Well, an inhabitant of the pond."

"A fish?"

"Probably…"

"Don't be ridiculous! Since when did fish get angry? Fish don't have minds."

"Yes they do!" he protested. "Even old clogs and cloths have minds," he continued bizarrely. "You all know about the maid who was found dead at the Director's house. The cause of death was found to be suffocation, but as to how she suffocated nobody knew. The fact is she died because she threw away a cloth that could still be used. The cloth got angry and jumped out at her when she came to put the rubbish out. It blocked her nose and mouth so that she couldn't breathe."

Eel looked so earnest when he said this that we began to put our clothes back on.

"If it means that much to you, we'll leave the pond alone."

Eel looked very happy.

"I thought you'd just laugh at me," he said. "But you really listened to what I said! I'd like to offer you all a meal! Please, come to my house!"

And he walked off briskly, leading the way.

His house was exactly halfway between the mine and the pond. He lived alone – although he was almost forty, he had no wife or children. The house was really not much more than a shack. The strangest thing was that it spanned a small river – not a clear fast-flowing stream, but a turgid, green stretch of water, flowing so slowly that it was difficult to detect any movement at all. One couldn't see to the bottom, but it looked very deep to me.

"This is a strange place to build a house," we said. "It must get very humid with that river underneath."

"Not as much as you'd think," said Eel. "And it's very convenient to be over a river."

"In what way?"

"For washing rice and vegetables," said Eel, "and dishes."

"And if you hung some hooks out you could catch some carp or eel," suggested one of us. "You could be quite self-sufficient."

"I don't like fish," declared Eel. "I only eat vegetables."

"Well, I can understand that," someone said. "If Eel was to eat eel, it'd be cannibalism!"

We all laughed, but Eel did not even smile. He opened his food cupboard and offered us some stewed potatoes.

"By the way, where does this river flow to?" someone asked. "Does it flow into the Hayase?"

The Hayase was the largest river in the vicinity. It flowed into the Sarugaishi, which then flowed on into Kitakami. All the small rivers and streams in the area flowed into the Hayase. So we expected him to say yes.

To our surprise he shook his head.

"It flows into that bottomless pond we were at earlier. We're higher here than the pond, of course."

"That's ridiculous," said one of us. "It's impossible. This river is three metres wide. If all the water in the river flowed into that pond, the pond would overflow."

Eel sneered. "I told you the pond was bottomless, didn't I?" he said. "So however much water comes in, it never overflows."

Eel was quite insistent about this, and his manner put us off. We soon left the house, without touching the potatoes.'

Inubuse reached for the kettle hanging over the hearth and filled a cup with hot water. He drank it very slowly, and then, turning back to me, resumed his story.

'One Saturday a few weeks later, the office manager asked me out to supper. He came over to my desk while I was working and asked quietly if I would like to come to his house that evening for some *sashimi* – he told me he had some squid that had been landed at Kamaishi that morning. I was rather suspicious, as we were not on particularly familiar terms, but I went along nevertheless, attracted by the prospect of squid *sashimi*. I think you'll agree that freshly caught squid *sashimi* is a real treat. It's not something you can experience anywhere but the Sanriku coast.

When we had drunk four or five flasks of *sake*, the manager suddenly lowered his voice.

"Inubuse, you're friendly with Numagishi aren't you. I'd just like to ask if you've noticed anything about him recently."

Numagishi was the accounts clerk with the featureless face, whom we called Eel.

"I'm not particularly close to Numagishi," I told him. "So I can't really say. Why do you ask?"

"Well..." The manager paused with his *sake* cup in front of his lips. He looked at me pensively. Then, in still more hushed tones, he spoke again.

"Numagishi is taking company money," he said. "The amounts are not large, and his job means he's responsible for bank deposits and withdrawals – so it wasn't noticed at first. But he's been taking five yen a month for the past two years."

"I don't believe it."

"It's a fact. So the company's looking into things. Do you think he might have a woman in Kamaishi, or Tono?"

"It's unthinkable. He lives the life of a monk. I've never heard him even talk about women."

"That's the most dangerous type," said the manager with a coarse glint in his eye. "The Director never talks about women either, but he's got two of them – one in Kamaishi and one in Tono. You know the market rate for keeping a woman in the pleasure quarters? Five yen a month – exactly what's being taken by Numagishi. It's quite a coincidence, isn't it? How about it, Inubuse? Do you fancy doing some detective work?"

"Detective work?"

"I'd like you to keep an eye on Numagishi for a while. Make a sudden visit to his house late at night – look for any signs of a woman. On Sundays he always goes to Kamaishi or Tono. Find out why."

"That's not detective work – that's just snooping."

"You'll benefit at your next pay raise. You'd normally be due a raise of fifty sen, but if you do this, you could get five times that – two yen fifty sen. What do you say, Inubuse? Will you do it?"

I didn't want to spy on a colleague, but I thought a blunt refusal of the manager's request would damage my prospects. I couldn't decide.

"Please give me until Monday to think about it," I said. "Of course, whether I do it or not, I won't mention the matter to anyone else."

That night and the following day I sat staring at the walls of my room. I thought and thought, but I reached no conclusion. At first it seemed to me I should refuse – it just didn't seem proper behaviour. On the other hand, I was worried about the consequences of refusal. The management was not to be trusted, and they could make my life very difficult. I certainly didn't want to resign; at that stage I intended to work at the mine all my life. So I began to think I should agree to do it for the sake of my future. But of course that didn't make it morally right. I thought the matter through again and again, but kept finding myself going in circles. Eventually tiring of this mental merry-go-round, I went out for a walk. Before I knew it, I found myself outside Numagishi's house on the river. I wasn't sure why I had gone there, but looking back I think I was driven by a slavish impulse to do my employer's will. Though I knew in my heart it wasn't right, my body was simply doing what the company wanted.

"Since I'm here," I said to myself, "I may as well call on Numagishi."

I knocked on the door. But there was no reply.

"He's out," I thought, and I was about to set off home again when I heard Numagishi's voice from the direction of the road.

"Here we are, Koi-san. This is my house."

"'Koi-san' – he's with a woman," I thought. So the manager was right. I tiptoed across to a bush in front of the house and hid.

"You'll be all right here," Numagishi was saying. "Nobody lives nearby, so there'll be no prying eyes. Take it easy for a while inside."

Numagishi was leading a woman by the hand. She was wearing a *yukata* robe tied with a red sash. She was in her early twenties and very beautiful.

When they reached the entrance she drew her hands together and bowed.

"I can never thank you enough!" she said to Numagishi. "If you hadn't paid that money I would now be in front of a group of drunkards in that room at Kiraku…"

Numagishi took her hand again and stroked it gently.

"Koi-san," he said. "Try to forget. You are free now. Be happy. That is all that matters."

The woman nodded cheerfully as Numagishi urged her into the house.

I knew that Kiraku was a large establishment in the Kamaishi pleasure quarters.

"So Koi is a *geisha*!" I thought, emerging slowly from the bush. "Numagishi must have rescued her from a difficult customer, which means he paid to release her from her establishment – with the company's money, of course."

My reaction seems odd to me even now. I felt invigorated. Here was an unattractive middle-aged man, who, while appearing to live the life of a monk, was not just a secret habitué of the pleasure quarters, but had gone so far as actually to redeem a geisha – the type of thing only a very rich man could do. His double life seemed to me quite splendid.

It was then that I thought of a third way to deal with my predicament. I could tell Numagishi that the company suspected his embezzlement and that he should get away at once. He could start afresh with his woman elsewhere. If I did this, I wouldn't be called a snoop, and if Numagishi ran off, the manager couldn't ask me to watch him.

So I knocked at the entrance.

"Numagishi!" I shouted.

"Who's that?" said Numagishi from inside. Naturally he sounded nervous.

"It's me. Inubuse."

The door opened slightly, revealing Numagishi's featureless face.

"Inubuse?" he said. "What do you want?"

"Your embezzlement has been discovered," I said. "You'd better get away."

He came outside.

"Is that true?" he said.

"Yes," I said. "If you don't act quickly you'll be caught."

"But why are you telling me?"

"The Director spends his money on women while we work as slaves. Your love life is as decadent as his – and you're doing it on his money. It makes me feel good. It's marvellous!"

"Me? Love life?" said Numagishi.

"There's no point hiding it," I said. "I saw you coming here with the beautiful Koi-san. I saw you going into the house together."

"Don't be ridiculous!" Numagishi opened the door wide. "There's nobody here. It was a koi *carp* I was with."

I looked into the house. There was no sign of anybody. It was just one room, and there was nowhere anybody could hide. But inside the entrance was a bucket of water with a carp splashing about inside.

"I went to Kamaishi today," said Numagishi. "As I was passing Kiraku I saw this carp about to be cooked. So I bought it. It's a strange thing about me that I can't stand to see a fish being killed."

I looked at him in amazement. He picked up the carp and threw it into the river. It flicked its tail with a splash and then disappeared down into the green water.

"That's strange. I definitely saw a woman."

"Just your imagination," he said, wiping his wet hands on his trousers.

"But," he continued, "it is true that I have been taking money. My hobby is buying carp and perch and setting them free here in the river. But I ran short of money so I helped myself to some from the company. It's a strange hobby, I admit… Anyway, thank you very much for telling me."

I went home feeling that a fox had pinched my nose. We never saw Numagishi again.'

The old man poured some more hot water into his cup from the kettle.

'It's very odd that you mistook a carp for a woman,' I said. 'There must have been something wrong with you.'

'Maybe,' said Inubuse, quietly placing his cup on the floor.

'There was a lot of gossip about Numagishi for a while,' he continued. 'But it gradually died down and he was forgotten about.

The Matsuo Shrine autumn festival came along and as usual we took our *sekihan* and *sake* and went out onto the hills behind the mine. When we were there somebody again suggested catching some fish in the pond.

"We gave up last time because of Numagishi, but now that he's not here…"

"Yes," said another. "Why don't we take all the water out to see if there's a bottom?"

We went straight off and fetched a pump from the mine and then rigged up some hoses to take the water from the pond to a nearby stream. When the level of the pond had dropped some way, a Buddhist priest came up to us and started sermonizing about the morality of what we were doing.

"Stop this pointless killing!" he said.

"It doesn't seem pointless to us," we said. "We're going to give the fish to the people in the village to liven up their supper. We don't think there's anything wrong in that."

"If you take out the water, all the fish will die at once, even the young ones that nobody will eat. It is a grave sin to destroy life. You mustn't do it!"

He was beginning to get on our nerves.

"Shut up, priest!" one of us said. "The pond belongs to the village. It's nothing to do with you."

"Here, have some *sekihan*," said another, passing him a food box. "Go away and eat it somewhere else."

The priest stood watching us for a while longer with the box in his hand. Eventually, he gave a deep sigh and said, "I see that since you are set on killing, there is nothing that I can do."

He plodded away.

We kept pumping for several hours, but still hadn't reached the bottom of the pond. It was beginning to get dark and we were growing tired of our experiment. It looked like it was going to take more than one day, but we had to go work in the morning.

But then suddenly somebody shouted.

"Look! I can see the bottom!"

We stopped pumping and looked. There, in the light of the setting sun, was the bottom of the pond. We stared and saw little waves splashing all around.

"How could there be waves there?" we thought, and looking more carefully saw that they weren't waves at all. They were eels and carp and a host of other fish wriggling and thrashing on the bottom of the pond.

"What's that slithering about in the middle?" shouted someone. "It looks like a log."

It wasn't a log. It was a huge writhing carp, thirty centimetres across and two-and-a-half metres long.

We had nets ready and everybody worked very hard pulling in the fish. It was the next morning by the time we finished. In all we got over fifty bucketfuls. Of course we pulled in the giant eel as well. Once it was up on the bank we looked at it carefully. We all shuddered when we saw its face.'

Inubuse was silent for a while.

'What was wrong?' I asked. 'Was there something strange about the giant eel?'

Eventually he nodded, slowly.

'Yes,' he said. 'The eel's face was very similar to that of our absent colleague, Numagishi.'

'I don't believe it!'

'It's true. And that's not all.'

'What else?'

'When we sliced the eel up, we found *sekihan* in its stomach.'

'*Sekihan*…? You're not saying that the itinerant priest who tried to stop you killing the fish was actually a giant eel?'

'He *was* a giant eel. There's no doubt about it. We found prayer beads and a priest's hat in the pond.'

'So you think that the eel-faced accountant, the itinerant priest, and the giant eel guardian of the pond were all the same person – or should I say the same eel?'

'There's no other possibility. Numagishi was the guardian of the pond. That was why he took company money to buy fish that were about to be killed. That was his mission as the guardian of the pond. He brought the fish that he saved back to his house and set them free in the river. From there they swam down to live peacefully in the pond.'

'That's ridiculous,' I said. 'Even if an eel were to have supernatural powers it wouldn't go and work in an office!'

'Whether you believe it is up to you,' said the old man, taking the lid off his box of *sekihan*. 'I've simply told you what happened – the facts of the case.'

'Oh!' he said, after a pause. 'I forgot to mention what occurred after that. The fortunes of the village rapidly declined. First, the mine's deposit of iron ore was exhausted. And then over the following year there was a series of disasters. The dynamite store exploded and there was a dysentery epidemic.'

Inubuse stuck his chopsticks into the *sekihan*.

'Apart from me, all the people who'd pumped the water from the pond were dead within the year. I survived because Numagishi remembered the help I'd given him – telling him that his embezzlement had been found out and that he should run away.'

Inubuse opened his box of *sekihan*. I opened mine too. I didn't have much of an appetite, though. I kept thinking of the *sekihan* found in the giant eel's stomach.

狐穴
Fox Hole

It was my third autumn working at the mountain sanatorium near Kamaishi, and I was thinking of resigning. Before coming to the sanatorium I had been studying at a private humanities university in Tokyo. When I left I had retained my registration 'just in case,' and had now written to the university asking to resume my studies. During my time at the sanatorium I had been saving money for fees and studying to enter medical school. But things had not gone as I had hoped. In the spring I had taken entrance exams for one national and one private medical school. The Japanese and English language exams were fine – even German was okay; the problem was mathematics. I found mathematics difficult to study on my own and at the end of the exams my answer papers remained whiter than the virgin peaks of the Himalayas. So I gave up on my brain and decided to return to my original university.

Nowadays, the art of medicine is often seen as a branch of the art of money-making; but in those days medicine was still regarded as an honourable calling. At the sanatorium I had been surrounded by tuberculosis patients and I felt a deep desire to help the sick. I felt that, as long as I could be a doctor, I wouldn't mind being poor for the rest of my life.

My philanthropy was of course immature, a sentimental priggishness common in young people – but nevertheless preferable to money worship. And if I may put my stupidity to one side for a moment, and stand up for myself a little, I would venture to suggest that the exam system whereby young people like me, who genuinely want to become doctors, are rejected because they do badly in a mathematics exam should, together with the current disgraceful practice of linking the award of places to size of donations, be fed to the pigs.

Or *is* trigonometry, for example, actually necessary in the performance of a surgical operation? 'Make a twelve-centimetre horizontal incision in the patient's abdomen below the navel from A to B. Cut six centimetres from point B to point C at a right angle to incision A–B. What is angle BCA? If it is thirty degrees or more then the stomach ulcer operation may be regarded as successful.' If such were the case then it would be reasonable when selecting potential doctors to put a great emphasis on the results of mathematics exams.

But what is actually required of those in the medical profession is quite different. One essential is quick and reliable manipulation of the surgical knife. (I have confidence in this. While no great cook, I'm extremely adept at chopping radishes. When we had a baseball camp at the sanatorium I chopped a number of giant radishes very quickly and with great precision. A young doctor who was captain of the team and played first base praised my astonishing speed.)

Doctors should also have strong nerves so that they do not drop their knife in distress at the sight of patients' blood, or faint when blood spurts onto their clothes. (I have no problem there. When I was a young boy my favourite pastime, shared with many of my fellows, was to catch a green frog, put a straw in its anus and carefully blow air in. We used to gamble with sweets and our honour on who could achieve the largest frog balloon. Never once did I faint, even when the frog exploded, its entrails splattering in all directions. Just from this example you can see how strong my nerves were. Perhaps it would be more accurate to say I had no nerves at all.)

A surgeon must also be able to identify at a glance whether an organ is, for example, the duodenum or the pancreas, based on a comparison between knowledge stored in their heads and the visual evidence of actual organs in front of them. (I was entirely confident on this score. On the night before high school graduation I'd had the opportunity of examining at close proximity a woman's private parts in a small dimly lit room in an entertainment district of Sendai City. Although in a state of what must be described as abnormal excitement, just one glance was sufficient for me fully to appreciate the relationship between what I then saw and the anatomical diagrams I had so frequently examined in the popular science books at a shop on my way home from school. It took but a moment to complete my comparison of the map, so to speak, with the actual landscape).

As you will appreciate from what I have written in brackets above I was material to be at least a doctor of some level, if not a fully fledged quack then perhaps at least some kind of quackling.

But to return to my narrative, in due course I received an official postcard from my university confirming that I could resume my studies and I immediately submitted my resignation to the head of the sanatorium. This was accepted without demur, the organisation having but a dim appreciation of my administrative skills. And thus, one September afternoon, I bade farewell to my colleagues in the office, to my boss, and to the head of the sanatorium, and, with a can of tempura oil bought that morning at a food store in Kamaishi, I set off for Inubuse's cave. The oil was a present for him. I was very grateful for all the stories he had told me over the previous two years, and for the escape from boredom these had provided. When I had asked him the previous day whether there was anything I could get him, he had replied immediately:

'A can of tempura oil. Living in a cave the whole time, my body gets cold – I couldn't carry on without a drop of oil from time to time.'

As I walked towards the cave I stopped several times to look around. Since I was going back to Tokyo, it would be some time before I saw this path again. I looked down at the grass at my feet and up at the mountainside. I suddenly noticed something strange. On the same slope as Inubuse's cave, there were seven or eight holes about fifty centimetres wide, each half-covered with grass.

'I've been to the cave at least once a week for the past two years,' I thought. 'Why haven't I noticed these holes before?'

I put the oil can on the ground and looked again at the mountainside. It seemed brighter than it had the previous week. I noticed some fresh-looking tree stumps, and next to them the trunks of pine trees lying on the grass.

They've been felling trees, I thought. *That explains the brightness. And the trees must have been hiding the holes.*

I picked up the oil again and walked on, with one eye still on the holes.

'They're fox holes,' said a voice in front of me. It was Inubuse. 'This used to be a fine residential area for foxes,' he told me as I reached the cave.

'Are they no longer here?'

'They all disappeared when rumours started about the sanatorium being built. They probably went to Mount Goyo.'

Mount Goyo is between Kamaishi and Ofunato. One thousand three hundred and forty-one metres high, it's the best-known mountain in the Kitakami range, and famous for deer and monkeys.

'It was fun when the foxes lived here,' said Inubuse. He went inside the cave and sat down cross-legged on the far side of the hearth. I sat on the near side, placing the can of tempura oil beside him.

'That's very kind,' he said, lifting his hand in gratitude. 'Thank you very much.'

'Why was it fun when the foxes were here?' I asked.

'Trapping them, for example,' he said. 'The best bait is a mouse cooked in tempura oil. There's nothing a fox likes better than mouse tempura. Foxes are normally wily creatures, but if you bait a trap with mouse tempura they'll walk straight in. It's very funny.'

Despite his words, his face looked sad.

'Foxes are lovely animals,' he said. 'You never get bored if there's a fox hole nearby. Sometimes they put on performances for people.'

'What kind of performances?'

'They appear in different guises – to keep people in the mountains amused.'

'I don't believe you.'

'Oh?' said the old man, looking very surprised. 'Why not?'

'It's always enjoyable to listen to you,' I said, 'but what you say doesn't always hang together.'

I took a notebook out of the back pocket of my trousers and turned the pages.

'I've written down all the stories you have told me in this notebook. Here, "The Pheasant Girl" – that's a totally unbelievable story. And anything you say about foxes pretending to be what they're not will be exactly like that – utterly unreal. Of course, I'm not criticising you. I'm very happy to *pretend* that it's true. Foxes appearing in different guises – that's fine with me.'

'What's unbelievable about "The Pheasant Girl"?'

The old man took the kettle from its hook above the hearth and poured some hot water into a cup. He blew on the hot water, his lips pushed forward like a fox's snout.

'How old are you?' I asked.

'Sixty-one or sixty-two, I think.'

'But in "The Pheasant Girl" you said the following: "In the great depression of 1926, the first year of the Showa era, my father was bankrupted. I was a high school student." That means you were twenty in about 1929 or 1930. And now it is 1955. If what you said in "The Pheasant Girl" is true you must now be forty-five or forty-six. Yet you just said you thought you were sixty-one or sixty-two.'

Inubuse grinned awkwardly as he sipped his hot water.

'And there are other things that don't tie up,' I continued. 'For example, "In the Pot"...'

'Stop there,' Inubuse said, putting his empty cup down with a clink on the edge of the hearth. 'Everything I have told you is true.'

'But...'

'If there are things that don't tie up, it's because I have only been showing part of myself. Today's your last day, so I'll tell you a story that shows every side of me. Then everything will tie up – probably.'

He rubbed his hands up and down his face for a while, deep in thought. Then in a quiet voice he started to talk.

'It happened during the war. We were on orders from the military to live in this area and collect pine roots. It was the last autumn of the war. The military wanted pine roots in order to make a type of turpentine which could be used as aircraft fuel. I was walking from the accommodation huts to the pine forest with the other workers…'

'…when a fox appeared in disguise…'

'Don't rush ahead!' he said with a rueful smile. 'I went to excuse myself,' he continued, 'and fell behind the rest of the group. I must have taken a wrong turning, because however far I walked I didn't catch them up, and I didn't reach the pine grove either. I walked for about two hours and was beginning to feel very tired and thirsty. Fortunately, there was a stream close by, so I went down to the stream and had a drink, washed my face, and took a rest. While I was there I noticed an unexpected sound. Through the constant babble of the stream, I heard the trundle of a spinning wheel.

"There must be a house nearby," I thought.

I walked up from the stream in the direction of the sound of the spinning wheel. A hundred metres up the hillside was a small area of flat land – about six hundred square metres. Right in the middle was a little house. Outside the house was a large spinning wheel, rotating slowly under the guidance of a pair of white hands.

"White hands!" I thought, staring at them, eagle-eyed. "Must be female."

Of that I was certain, but unfortunately, her face was hidden. I couldn't tell whether she was young or old – adult or child.

"May I ask you something?" I said loudly as I walked towards the spinning wheel. "I think there's a place for digging pine roots near here. Do you know how to get there?"

I was about ten metres away when the seated figure suddenly raised her head. She was a lovely woman of about twenty-six or twenty-seven, with pale skin and an oval face. Her hair was coiled loosely on top of her head. Her long narrow eyes smiled at me.

"You'll have to go over the hilltop behind me."

She had a remarkable voice. It was cheerful and vivacious, but at the same time somehow smooth and moist. It had a voluptuous quality which, to put it coarsely, appealed to a man's nether regions.

"Go over the top of the hill," she said, "and walk down for two hundred metres and you'll be there."

She lifted one hand from the spinning wheel and held it in front of her mouth, laughing softly. I didn't know what was amusing.

"What's so funny?" I said. "Are there leaves on my face or something?"

"No," she said waving her white fingers. "I was just thinking what beautiful big nuts…"

She started to titter again.

I was astonished. Her gaze seemed to be wandering over the crotch of my trousers.

I was in my prime in those days and my spirit rose valiantly to the occasion.

"I am honoured by your observation, madam," I said, "but my nuts are not simply well-formed. The women of the valleys say they taste as good as they look."

It puts me in a cold sweat to think that I spoke like that to a woman I'd never met before, but that's exactly what I did. Her white face was suddenly touched with the red tints of autumn.

"Ooh!" she said, laughing more shrilly. "I'm not talking about your nuts. I'm talking about the nuts on the tree beside you."

I turned and saw full pods hanging heavily from the boughs. I took one pod, slit it open, and gave her a handful of smooth plump nuts.

"I'm sorry," I said.

I ran red-faced up the hill behind her house. I soon found the pine-root diggers on the far side.

"I've just met an amazingly beautiful woman on the other side of this hill," I announced immediately.

"It's her time of year already, is it?' chuckled an old man called Sho.

"Her time of year?" I said. "What do you mean? Do you know her?"

"Yes I do," he said. "I've been to these mountains many times before. That woman's famous around here!"

"Is there a reason…?"

"There certainly is!" he said chuckling again. "That 'woman' is not a woman at all. She's a fox."

When I thought about it, it certainly did seem strange that out there – half a day from Kamaishi and a whole day from Tono – there would be a beautiful woman living alone in the mountains. It was also odd that she hadn't shown the slightest caution with a complete stranger. And it was, to say the least, lacking in female modesty to stare so brazenly at a man's crotch as he walked towards her. Perhaps she was a fox after all, just as Sho said.'

'So what happened with this fox-woman?' I asked Inubuse. 'Or is that the end of the story?'

'Be patient,' he said, raising his palms to calm me. 'That's just the start. One evening a few days later, we were permitted to go down from the mountain. In those days everybody – the soldiers at the front and the people back in Japan – were supposed to stay at their posts every day without a break until our "Holy War" had brought victory. The government had slogans like "Monday, Monday, Tuesday, Wednesday, Thursday, Friday, Friday." But here in the mountains, a long way from anywhere, we were allowed the luxury of one day off in ten to go home and take things easy.'

As I listened to Inubuse talk I picked up some tongs and traced the character for 'fox', 狐, several times in the ashes of the hearth. Outside the cave, an autumnal breeze rustled through the pampas grass.

'I left our hut at about four in the afternoon,' said Inubuse. The autumn sun sets early and I wanted to reach the village of Kosano on the outskirts of Kamaishi before dark, so I walked at quite a pace. Most of my workmates had left earlier, and I was completely alone. A mountain path on an autumn evening appeals to poetic sensibilities, but it can also be unnerving. On that occasion, I found myself beset by a strange sense of fear, which to my shame almost impelled me to run.

When I had been on the path for about an hour, I came to a forest of pampas grass. Of course, one wouldn't normally say a "forest" of pampas grass, but since the pampas grass around here grows taller than a man, the word "forest" conveys a reasonable impression. Just as I reached the forest I was relieved to hear some voices ahead of me. Thinking I might walk with them as far as Kosano I hurried forward until they were in view. There was a man and a woman. The woman had a long white neck and her hair was coiled casually above her head. I recognized her. She was the woman at the spinning wheel. The man was speaking. His voice sounded young:

"I've come from Ofunato and I want to get to Kamaishi as quickly as I can. This road goes through Kosano, doesn't it? I got detailed directions in Ofunato but I was beginning to feel uneasy. I saw you ahead of me so I thought I'd check…"

"You'll get to Kosano if you keep on this path," replied the woman in her smooth, moist tone. "Another two hours and you'll see the lights of the village."

"What a relief!" the man said, unfolding a hand towel and wiping the sweat from his face. His movements seemed more graceful than those of the local men.

"My house is about thirty minutes from here," the woman said, looking up at him. "Shall I walk with you until we get there?"

I was about fifty metres from them, but even at that distance, I could feel the power of her seductive eyes.

"I wouldn't like to impose on you, though," she added.

"I would be delighted," said the man. "It would be a great honour to walk with such a beautiful lady, even for just thirty minutes."

They walked on together. I followed. I had two reasons for not joining them. Firstly I was inhibited but the intimacy between them, one that seemed remarkable in people who had only just met. Secondly, I was interested to find out why the woman had told a lie about her house being thirty minutes' walk away.

"Why are you going to Kamaishi?" she asked the man, looking up into his face as they walked slowly along. "I suppose there must be a pretty girl waiting for you there. How vexing!"

"You must be joking," said the man, stopping to light a match for his cigarette. "I'm going to see my sister, who's married to a manager at the Kamaishi Iron Works. I left Ofunato a day earlier than my friends to get a chance to see her again."

The woman shielded the match for him with her hands. The man squeezed them gently as he lit his cigarette. He inhaled contentedly and started to walk again, boldly keeping one of her hands in his.

"Your friends?" she said.

"Yes. We're a troupe of travelling actors. We've been performing in Sendai, Ishinomaki, Onagawa, Kesennuma, and Ofunato. Today is a very rare day off. The others are resting in Ofunato.

"So you're an actor?"

"Well, yes."

"That's why you are so handsome. No wonder I was tongue-tied when I saw you."

The man stopped. Still clasping her hand, he looked her straight in the face.

"If you speak like that," he said, throwing his cigarette to the ground, "I shall take you seriously! People might laugh to hear me say this – I've known you for less than half an hour after all – yet, how can I put it? I…"

"Say no more," the woman said, gently freeing her hand from his. "It does not do to talk plainly of matters between a man and a woman."

She lifted her hand and placed it over his mouth.

"I live alone. I shall make you some tea, and then we can slowly…"

"Slowly…?"

"Yes. Do what a man and woman who are together will always… Slowly and to our hearts' content."

The woman pointed down the path.

"We're almost at my house," she said. "It is not five minutes away. If we did that sort of thing out here we'd cut ourselves. Pampas grass and reeds are as sharp as blades."

"So… you will *accommodate* me?"

"Certainly I shall! Stay the whole night if you can. But, of course, you're going to your sister's house."

"Oh, don't worry about her!"

The woman nodded happily. This time she took his hand firmly in hers and tugged him towards the house.

"Extraordinary!" I thought as looked at the house. This was a path I walked quite frequently and I thought I knew it well. I felt certain there had been no house in the pampas grass forest. All I had noticed before was a small cesspit, used for fertilising a rice field that a farmer from Kosano had cleared in the forest.

I approached the house quietly. It was a typical well-ordered farmhouse. Freshly peeled persimmons were hanging from the eaves like a reed blind. Chickens were clucking around the garden, pecking feed from the ground. A black cat was sprawled on the veranda. Its eyes flashed as I approached. This was not a house that had been erected overnight.

"It must have been here all along," I thought. "I just didn't notice it."

As I drew closer to the veranda, I heard the woman's voice from inside the house.

"Here we are! Now, first you must have some tea."

I knelt on the veranda and, leaning forward on my left hand, I put the forefinger of my right hand into my mouth to wet it with spittle. I then pressed it against the paper *shoji* screen that separated the veranda from the inside of the house. A moment's pressure and *zubu!* My finger slipped through the paper.

I pulled my finger back and gently put my right eye against the hole. Peering this way and that, I gradually built up a picture of what lay beyond the screen. My jaw slowly dropped.'

Inubuse set his cup down firmly on the floor.

'I was truly astonished,' he said.

'What? What did you see?' I said. My voice was strangely hoarse – listening with rapt attention to the story, my mouth had become extremely dry.

'Inside the screen,' he said, 'was a pampas grass forest.'

As usual the old man made a ceremony of slowly filling his pipe with cut tobacco and lighting it from the hearth.

'In other words,' he said, 'beyond the screen there was no building. It was open land.'

He exhaled purple smoke.

'And…?' I said.

'Below the hem of the woman's kimono was something brown and furry – a tail.'

'So she was a fox then.'

'That's right. Of course the tail was behind the woman, so the man couldn't see it.'

'And…?'

'The man was holding a strange vessel made of bamboo grass. He lifted it to eye-level.

"This is no ordinary tea cup," he said, rotating it solemnly. "In my view this must surely be a cup of the greatest distinction."

"What fine taste you have!" said the woman, smiling happily.

At that moment her mouth opened as far as her ears. It lasted only an instant, but I saw it quite clearly.

"That is a piece by Bambuemon,' she said.

"Bambuemon…?"

"A pupil of the famous Persiemon'

"Ah! Well! I see!" he said pompously.

I struggled to contain my laughter. "Ah! Well!" he says. Well and truly fallen for it! "I see!" he says. He couldn't see beyond the end of his nose!

"Another cup of tea?" asked the woman.

"Yes please," said the man, holding the bamboo grass cup up to the woman's eyes.

"I'm very thirsty after my long walk. Please fill it right up."

"Of course," said the woman, and sank a ladle down beside her. Looking carefully, I saw that she had plunged it into a small cesspit. She stirred the slopping contents of the cesspit, then lifting the ladle carefully up she filled the man's bamboo leaf cup.

"What a beautiful fragrance!" he said. His eyes were closed in rapture. He took one deep breath and drank the contents in a single draught.

Through the hole in the screen I could clearly see that he was kneeling on bare ground under an open sky, that the cup was bamboo grass, that the teapot was a ladle, and that the tea was human excrement. The man was entirely under the fox's spell – he thought he was in a fine room enjoying tea with a beautiful woman. I felt sad for him in a way. It occurred to me to shout to the man and so break the fox's spell, but one doesn't often get the opportunity to see a fox pretending to be human. So I managed to control my charitable instinct, and carried on watching.

"Ah! I've just remembered," said the woman, twisting around. "I have some *manju* cakes from Nishikiya."

Behind her was a tree stump on top of which lay several pieces of dried horse dung.

"Do have some!" she said, picking one up and holding it under the man's nose. "It's a famous delicacy of Kamaishi,"

Though I had lived in Kamaishi for over twenty years, I had never come across a shop called Nishikiya.

"Nothing's going to stop this fox!" I thought. "She's just saying whatever comes into her head."

"Thank you!" said the man, taking the dung. "Hmm, it's the colour of horse manure."

"That's why its other name is *Man'yu Manju*. But it's delicious. Not too sweet."

"Let me try..." He closed his mouth over the dung. He chewed and chewed, and eventually swallowed.

'Excellent!" he said, smacking his lips.

"Have another!" said the woman.

But as she twisted around again to get more dung, the man leapt at her and tried to hold her down.

"That's enough *manju*," he said. "Now for a taste of something else."

"You're so rough! Grabbing me like that!" she cried, and slipping from his arms, ran off to the left. Of course she was only teasing him and had no real intention of escaping.

"You know what you promised!" said the man, chasing her. The woman screamed and fell over on the grass.

"There! Got you!" he said.

At last the man was on top of the woman – or that's what *he* thought, but I suppose it would be more accurate to say the man was on top of the fox.

"Ahh!" the woman cried as they struggled. "Are you really human?"

The man, who was fumbling to remove his trousers, froze.

"What do you mean?"

"I just touched it. It's so long and thick. You must be a horse, pretending to be human!"

"Of course I'm human – there's no question about it."

"I'm not so sure."

"Mm," said the man, smiling ironically. "I think it's *you* that's not human!"

"Why? What makes you say that?" she said in alarm, hurriedly closing her splayed legs.

"You're so keen to have a man take you. It makes me wonder."

"This is getting interesting," I thought. I'd known for a long time the woman was a fox, but the idea that the man might actually be a horse was a fresh development. If the woman was right, then here were a fox and a horse tricking each other – it might only happen once or twice in a thousand years.

Wishing to get the best possible view of this bout of the century, I licked my forefinger once more and pressed it against the paper screen to widen the hole. But the operation did not go as smoothly as it had the first time. Somehow the paper now seemed as tough as leather. I tried instead to make the hole bigger by scratching it, and then…

"Inubuse! What are you doing?" I heard a voice behind me.

I turned around to find my workmate Sho.

"Inubuse. What are you scratching there for?"

"Shh!" I gestured at him to be quiet.

"On the other side of this screen a fox is seducing a traveller – and the traveller may well be a horse."

"What are you talking about?" said Sho, bursting into laughter. "Where is this screen, Inubuse? You're scratching a horse's anus."

At first I thought Sho had gone mad. What about the garden, the clucking hens, the sprawling cat? I'd seen them all with my own eyes – I'd heard the hens with my own ears. What was wrong with Sho? Couldn't he see them? Couldn't he hear? And to say that the paper screen was a horse's rear was crazy.

But when I turned back to the screen, I realized immediately that Sho was right. What was in front of my eye was indeed a horse's rear. And of course, as soon as I realized that, the garden, the hens, the cat, the persimmons, and the house itself all disappeared. There was nothing but pampas grass rustling in the wind. Some distance away a farmer was cutting pampas grass. The horse must have belonged to him…'

Hearing what had really happened to Inubuse, I could control myself no longer and burst out laughing.

'You were completely fooled by the fox,' I said.

'That's right,' said Inubuse, grimacing and scratching his head. 'Everything, the traveller included, was a fabrication by the fox. I had been looking into a horse's anus the entire time.'

'You were lucky not to be kicked,' I said.

'I suppose you're right,' he said. 'That's something to be grateful for.'

Inubuse poured some more hot water into his cup.

'I've really learnt my lesson,' he said. 'Whenever I see a woman on an autumn path, I always wonder whether she's real.'

He drank the hot water, sipping it up slowly onto his tongue. Weak with laughter I looked out of the cave. The pampas grass was still swaying in the wind. For a moment I thought I saw a woman cross quickly through the pampas grass, but I am sure that was just my imagination, stirred up by listening to Inubuse's story.

'Well,' he said. 'That's the story. It wasn't much, but it had all of me in it.'

He reached for his trumpet, which was lying on his bedding at the back of the cave.

'I'd like to give you this. It's made by Horner's in Germany. It's not a great instrument, but it's not at all bad.'

'I can't possibly accept such a valuable thing,' I said, pushing it back to him. 'Besides, I have no ear for music, and I'm not interested in instruments. What I would like is to know what you mean when you say that the story had all of you in it. I don't understand at all. All the contradictions are still there. None of my questions about "The Pheasant Girl" have been settled. And why is it that you blow your trumpet every lunchtime anyway?'

'Try blowing it yourself and see,' Inubuse said, his eyes twinkling. 'The whole puzzle will be solved. Take it. Imagine that you've been fooled by a fox, and blow.'

He spoke firmly and I allowed myself to be persuaded. As I put my lips to the mouthpiece, I noticed a faint smell of pine resin. I blew, but of course no sound came out.

'Pucker your lips more,' he said, and puckered his own, pushing his mouth forward so that it resembled the long snout of a fox.

'Blow hard,' he said. 'Keep blowing!'

I blew hard again and again just as he told me, until I was out of breath, and a white mist formed in front of my eyes.

'Hey!' said a dry voice behind me. 'What are you sitting there for with a pine stick in your mouth?'

I turned around and saw a middle-aged man with a sheaf of mountain grass on his back. His round face was framed by a dirty towel tied under his chin.

'I'm not blowing a pine stick! I'm blowing a Horner…'

I closed my mouth. The man was right. What I had in my mouth was not a trumpet but a pine stick. Astonished, I looked around for Inubuse but he was not to be seen. There was just a fox hole almost overgrown with grass.

'You've been tricked, haven't you,' said the man, untying the towel and wiping the sweat from his face. 'Have you lost anything?'

'One can of tempura oil,' I said, getting up slowly. 'And a little time…'

'Tempura oil?' said the man. 'That must be Gengoro. He's the chief fox round here. He loves tempura oil. I thought he'd left for Mount Goyo a long time ago, but it looks like he's still prowling around here. I'll put a trap out this evening.'

The man tied the towel again around his face and set off downhill in the direction of the sanatorium, the mountain grass swaying on his back. I felt like flinging the pine stick down onto the fox hole. But then I thought better of it, and held the stick tight.

'If you were a fox, then it all makes sense,' I murmured. A wind swept down the mountainside, rustling through the pampas grass forest.

Glossary and Notes

Azuki beans (Vigna angularis). Small beans normally of a reddish colour, often used in Japanese cooking.

Biwa. A short-necked fretted lute, used traditionally to accompany certain kinds of storytelling.

Chan. An affectionate suffix used with names and abbreviated names.

Great Kanto Earthquake (1923). The most destructive earthquake in Japan's history, with the highest death toll (due also to the ensuing fires) and until 2011 the highest recorded magnitude. The Kanto region includes Tokyo and Yokohama, both of which were very badly affected by the earthquake.

Inari. A Shinto deity associated with foxes.

Jizo. A Bodhisattva (one category of enlightened being in Buddhism) often depicted as a child monk. *Jizo* is a protector of women, children and travellers. *Jizo* statues are common on pathways, roadsides and crossroads in Japan.

Kappa. Literally 'river child'. A supernatural, often malevolent creature, associated with ponds and rivers, and figuring in many folktales.

Kombu. Edible kelp, often used for flavouring.

Manju. A traditional confection, usually in the form of a small bun, often baked or steamed and with a sweet bean-paste filling.

Miyazawa Kenji (1896–1933). A much loved poet and writer of children's stories, he is a native of Iwate Prefecture, where he lived most of his life.

Mochi. Pounded rice cake.

O-kaeri nasai. 'Welcome home!' An everyday greeting.
Ozuchi. The name of this port a short way north of Kamaishi is normally rendered 'Otsuchi' in English. Inoue's text, however, specifies a 'z' pronunciation rather than 'ts' for the first consonant, so the name appears as 'Ozuchi' in this translation.
Sashimi. Thinly sliced fish (or meat) served raw.
Sekihan. Literally 'red rice'. Rice boiled with *azuki* beans: a traditional dish, often eaten on celebratory occasions.
Sen. One hundredth of a yen. Taken out of circulation in 1953.
Shiba. A small spitz-type dog, one of the six officially recognized breeds of Japanese 'native' dog. Still very popular in Japan.
Shochu. A strong alcoholic beverage, comparable to whisky, distilled (not brewed, like *sake*) from a variety of materials including rice, buckwheat, barley, sweet potatoes and even chestnuts.
Yukata. A cotton robe used in summer, and for sleeping.

Japanese Historical Periods

Edo 1603–1868
Meiji 1868–1912
Taisho 1912–1926
Showa 1926–1989

Readings of Japanese Characters Used in the Text

Headings

鍋の中	*nabe no naka*	In the Pot
川上の家	*kawakami no ie*	House up the River
雉子娘	*kiji-musume*	Pheasant Girl
馬	*uma*	Horse
狐	*kitsune*	Fox
話売り	*hanashi-uri*	Story Seller
沼	*numa*	Lake
鰻	*unagi*	Eel
狐穴	*kitsune-ana*	Fox Hole

In 'Fox'

針	*hari*	Needle

www.ingramcontent.com/pod-product-compliance
Lightning Source LLC
Jackson TN
JSHW020021141224
75386JS00025B/640

* 9 7 8 0 8 5 7 2 8 1 3 0 2 *